BEAUTY'S CURSE

PART I OF THE *ONCE UPON A PRINCESS* SAGA

☼   ☼   ☼   ☼

C. S. Johnson

Print ISBN: 978-1-943934-25-6
eBook ISBN: 978-1-943934-24-9

For all my kids at school–Brooks, Nolan, Rebekah, Satori, Mary, Andres, and Tyler, as well as Miles, Tate, Sam, and, for this one, especially Ethan–I taught in hopes you would learn to be brave, and you ended up giving me the courage I needed to write something new. You know how much I love irony. Thank you for making such a difference in my life.

This is also for another Sam. While this is not the usual story you've heard, you're too much of my own for me not to be grateful for you.

This book is published courtesy of

www.direwolfbooks.com

DIREWOLF
—— BOOKS ——

To Get *Awakening* (A Special Christmas Episode of The *Starlight Chronicles*) as a bonus for picking up this book,

Click Here

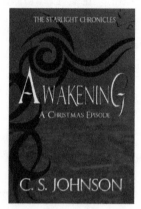

Or Download It At:
https://www.csjohnson.me/awakening

Prologue

⁙

"Get up."

It was the pain in his uncle's voice, rather than the urgency, which forced sleep from Theo's eyes. A sense of warning immediately pressed into him, sinking his body into the hard surface of his sleeping pad, even as he sought for the strength to crawl out of it.

"Get up, boy," the command barked out again, this time accompanied by a shaking hand dripping with the warmth of blood. "Your brother's already getting the horses ready."

Theo felt the sense of warning flare into danger as the new information began to piece itself together inside his seven-year-old mind. Not only was it unusual for Thaddeus, his older brother, to be up before the sun, but ever since the hostile fairyfolk of Riverbed Valley had overtaken the mountainside, no one in all of the kingdom of Rhone thought it wise to ride without the protection of daylight.

Flames spurt out from the other room as Theo hurried to get his things together. While his feet were quick to take him across the small cabin his father and uncle had built together, the one his mother had furnished with her love as much as her embroidery, Theo's heart pounded only with the desire for time to stand still. The call to remember everything, every little detail of his home beat inside of him as a resounding instinct. It rippled through his body, from his heart to his mind, distorting time and perception.

How strange his hand should shake, as he grabbed at the small bread packets, tucked away in their usual cabinet. How

1

had he never noticed the slump in the floors from the years of walking? Theo glanced at his Uncle Thom, wondering what could have happened, what could be so important at this time of night. But before he could say a word, he nearly stumbled at the sight of his uncle and his wounds.

Deep gashes, down both his arms and across his back, were surging rather than slipping with blood. Cuts and bruises were settled into the ebony of his beard.

"Uncle Thom," Theo gasped.

His uncle, always seemingly so fiery and strong, narrowed his gaze. "We don't have time to worry about it," he said, dismissing his battle wounds with an eerie calmness.

"But we have to get you some bandages," Theo insisted.

"We'll have to worry about it after we get to the church," Uncle Thom muttered, stoking the small flames of the fire. "Bring me your mother's tapestry, the one hanging there. And hurry."

Theo rushed over and prudently pulled down the tapestry; his mother had told him, long ago, how his father had won in one of his many successful tournaments, and given it to her. Woven into it was a scene from the legend of Queen Lucia, the Fairy Queen who fell in love with a mortal man, and had him prove his love and his worth by becoming a knight in her kingdom. Since then—or since the legend came about—it was said only those who were worthy of love and power would become knights. It was a favorite bedtime story of Theo's, and his mother indulged him so often with the tale, the landscape of his dreams often wove itself right into the tapestry, as he became a powerful knight and protected the kingdom like his father and uncle.

He carefully handed it over to his uncle, secretly hoping they would be able to wash out the bloodstains from his

ONCE UPON A PRINCESS

uncle's hands later. The selfish wish twisted into pain when his uncle began to tear it into strips.

"Wha–" Theo sputtered. "What are you doing? I thought you said we would take care of your wounds when we got to the church."

"This is not for me." Uncle Thom shook his head. "We have to destroy this, Theo," he said. He tossed some of the strips into the fire. "Look."

Theo would have rather shoveled out the stables than watch as the beautiful, blue-green eyes of the fairy Queen began to burn red. But curiosity got the better of him; he turned to face the fire. He blinked in surprise. The fire was burning green and pink sparks, like live flowers sprouting into flames.

"That," Uncle Thom explained, "is Magdust."

Theo stilled; suddenly, he knew. "Mother and Father are dead, aren't they?"

His uncle furrowed his brow. "It's complicated, Theo. But I'm sorry."

Theo grabbed the rest of the tapestry remnants from his uncle's hands and threw them into the fireplace. The scenery from his dreams fueled the fire and lit up the room, burning into reality and changing it all into a nightmare.

Then, bravely but uncertainly, he turned around on his heel, pushed the wayward tresses of his black hair back from his face, and marched out of the door.

At the freshness of the air, tears threatened to flow even more sharply, and he had to hide his face; for a long moment, he tried to pull himself together, even as his world and his home fell apart.

A hand on his back and a horse's snort jolted his hands off his face, allowing him to see his brother. Thad was looking down at him, his eyes colored with the same dark green determination; it was a heritage only a brother could share.

"Uncle Thom said we were to ride together," Thad told him. "You ride in the back, okay?"

Theo nodded. There was nothing else to do but follow orders; he would later think it was a small blessing in its own way, since he was unable to think of what had to be done himself.

"Hopefully, Butterscotch won't mind holding both of us," Thad said.

He is trying to comfort me, Theo understood bitterly. Thad was suddenly, at ten years of age, the leader in their home. And, Theo realized, that made him a burden. Before he could respond to his brother, the door to their house slammed shut for the last time as their uncle walked out.

In the soft morning light, creeping its way over the far mountains, Theo's hope crumbled. It was one thing to see his house burn, and his dreams destroyed; but it was entirely another to see his beloved uncle, his father's protector and best friend, stripped of his invincibility, slinking toward the outskirts of death.

In muffled curses and moans, Uncle Thom clambered onto his steed and came up beside them. "No matter what, boys," he said, "you will need to ride on to the church outside Havilah, the capital. I have a letter for them here," he said, sliding a rolled up and sealed message into the bounds of their horse's saddle. "No matter what, see they get it, and your grandfather will see to it that they take you in."

Thad and Theo both started to object, but with a wave of his hand, Uncle Thom commanded their attention once more.

"The fairies are after us," he intoned. "You need to get to the church. They have protection there. While we are in the forest, *do not* make a sound. For spies and sprites, commanded by that demon witch, Magdalina, are everywhere, and anywhere outside the church's ground is fair game to them. If they hear us, they will kill us."

"Like they killed our parents?" Thad asked, the anger cool but clear in his voice.

"Not quite," Uncle Thom said with a sigh. "I imagine it would be much worse for us." At Thad and Theo's stunned and confused silence, he nodded forward. "Be brave," he called, giving one last battle cry, as he kicked his heels and his horse sped off. Thad, sure of Theo's riding skill, hastened to set a close course behind him.

⁙

The wind whipped through Theo's hair, almost in a comforting way. But however well-meaning the wind, it only stirred the angry fires inside of him. As the trees flew by in passing, as the fairies nipped and brushed and bounced about in a hovering threat, as the monks and nuns hurried around the hallowed grounds of the church … as the last of his uncle's weakened confessions fell silent, Theo felt the rage burn on inside of him, into his skin and into his soul, marking him with a lonely fierceness and an empty, nameless hunger.

* * *

PART I

"Come away! O human child!
To the waters and the wild,
With a fairy hand-in-hand,
For the world's more full of weeping than you can
understand."

~ "The Stolen Child," Yeats

"Be strong and courageous. Do not be afraid; do not be
discouraged, for the Lord your God will be with you
wherever you go."

~ Joshua 1:9, NIV

1

:'.

She had never been one to waste her time; after all, she had so little of it left. But whether or not the weather cooperated with her was another matter entirely.

Rose looked up at the bleak sky, feeling the hood of her protective cloak sliding down from her face, exposing her nape at the end of her close-cropped hair. The wind tickled her skin, and rather than finding it charming and pleasant as she might have when she was younger, she found it taunting and terrifying.

Her gaze moved down from the crying skies to the sea, the rough and tumbling creature so keen on hogging every inch it could of the world's edge.

There was nothing to it, she decided. They would have to enter into the cavern during the rain. According to the map Ethan had found, the entrance to Titania's realm was not far down the cliff, and while it would be easier if the rain would stop and the tide would recede, Rose knew she could never count on life to make things easier for her if it could.

That was how Theo found her; looking down the edge of the cliffs, standing in the rain, and declaring all the world her enemy. No wonder she had insisted leaving the palace when she'd been thirteen, he thought. Even the grand palace would have demolished itself, had she been unable to fight her own way free of it. She was a warrior through and through.

Theo shook his head and pushed back the cover of his cloak. "I know that look," he muttered, coming up from behind her. "And the answer is no."

9

Rose would have normally grinned at the sight of her best friend following her out of the safety of the camp to talk. But ever since she and her group had finally found the location of the home of a powerful Fairy Queen, time seemed to crush into her a little bit more each day, pushing her into possible tomorrows long before her today's had finished.

She pursed her lips together. "Come on. I'm the princess, remember? I'm the one in command here, Theo."

He smiled at her. "You only pull rank when you know I'm right." Crossing his arms, he added, "It's only been two days, Rosary. We'll give it at least one more before we go barreling in."

He was not fooled by the calm look on her face; there would be a battle in getting her to agree.

He had known Rose–officially Princess Aurora Rosemarie Mohanagan of Rhone–for over ten years, ever since he arrived to work in the royal chapel, and he knew well her charms. It was impossible not to notice them, and knowing her well enough, it was impossible for him to fall for them– which, he knew, she both liked and hated on different occasions. Knowing her expressions just as well, Theo knew this time she hated it.

"Mary can protect us with a weather spell," she argued.

He had to admit, halfway begrudgingly, he admired her tenacity as she refused to back down. "Mary is still tired from our battle with the Eastern Warlords. We're all still tired, even you. The rest will be good for us. We have time enough for rest."

"No, I don't have time, Theo. My birthday is coming up." Frustration and fear crept into the pattern of her speech.

"And you can spare a day now, and we'll make up for it later."

"What if we don't?"

"You still have a whole year afterwards, Rosary." Patience melted away into concern at her words. He knew she was upset and afraid, and there was little he could do about it.

That was why he had come, though, wasn't it? The thought hit him with a disgruntled air. There were few reasons besides counsel and comfort that would cause one to bring a priest across continents and into battle. He was fortunate to have found a friend in the doomed princess of Rhone.

Theo watched as she started pacing, her knight's armor clanking quietly in tune with her stride. Time to reinforce the reason, he decided. "Sophia can't build much of a raft by the day's end. Why not send her to town with Virtue and some of the guards? She can surely go unnoticed here, even with your beast of a hawk, and she'll be able to see about a boat for tomorrow."

After a moment of silence, Rose smirked despite herself. "You and your logic," she muttered. She gave him a friendly punch on the shoulder. "Is there anything you don't use it for?"

"Some things," he replied, "that you know of well, and we share."

Rose felt a world pass between them inside his soft-spoken words, and found comfort in it. "Wanting revenge does tend to bind people together," Rose agreed, finally stopping in her tracks. She laid out her cloak and sat down on the ground. She pulled off her gloves, running her hands along the mossy ground. "Even people like you and me."

"You mean a princess and an orphan?"

She thought about it. "No, more than that," she said. "Not just that. More like someone cursed and someone raised by the church. But I guess that's wrong, too. You're not a priest. Not yet, anyway."

"All of mankind is cursed," Theo replied easily enough, sitting down next to her.

"I guess you sound like enough of one it's easy to forget," she teased back. She sighed. "It's not fair."

He looked over at her, and not for the first time, felt the pull of her presence. She was beautiful, even as she desperately tried to hide it. He didn't have the heart to tell her it was a waste of her time. With her chopped hair, the sunlight-kissed locks fluttered playfully, mysteriously; her eyes, as blue as the sky and unfathomable the sea, were framed by thick, sable lashes, and her lips, lips said to shame the reddest of roses, were as expressive and quirky as he knew her mind to be. Yes, he thought, life was not fair, even to the brightest among us.

Theo knew, having spent his adolescence in the palace, while Rose was angry at the curse placed on her at birth by the wicked fairy Magdalina, it was not the fear of a sleeping death that ailed her so much as the curse of relentless beauty. He smiled, recalling the day when an intended suitor, praising her with a song of her looks, had finally caused her perfected façade to fold.

Rose caught his smile. "What?" she snapped.

"I was thinking about the Prince of Crete," he said. "When he came, and you took his instrument—what was it? A mandolin or something?—and bashed him over the head with it, saying he should be ashamed he'd forgotten to mention how the pearly gates gleamed second only to your smile."

Rose laughed. "You remember his face? It was so red, I thought he was going to throw up."

"He looked like he'd just swallowed some pig slaw," Theo agreed. "But it was your mother's face which I still picture the best. She looked like she was going to murder you."

Rose giggled. "I guess that's one upside to Magdalina's curse. It's not like my mother's going to get away with murdering me. And neither will anyone else."

They fell back into an easy silence for a moment. Then Theo asked, "Is that why you like playing the mercenary knight?"

"It's not for just that reason," Rose assured him. She narrowed her gaze slyly in his direction. "You need the practice, remember?"

"Oh, I see now." Theo shook his head, trying to hide his grin. "Here I thought I was getting pretty good at being your squire."

"I told you months ago you were good enough to be a Rhonian knight," Rose reminded him. "Or did you just want to hear me say it again?"

"No, I wanted to hear you admit I'd beaten you in your battle testing." Theo smirked.

"Ha, it's always a riot with you. But anyway, Sophia's my official squire now."

"When she's not working on your armory."

"She likes doing that. And you know blacksmithing is very important to knights like us. She might as well practice and put it to use."

"She has been, and probably too much to really get in any knight training with the tournaments and the Eastern Warlord battles we've had recently."

"Which we might not have had to fight at all, if the Lead General hadn't been so demanding." Rose squeezed a handful of dirt and watched it slip through her fingers, a

13

mixture of dust and mud. "The people in Greece are already taxed enough. He had some nerve demanding more. Even people like Ethan and Sophia's family deserve better."

Theo nodded. "And you work for it. One way or another."

"I like fighting, but I would rather see justice done, whether it's on the battlefield or in diplomacy," Rose said. "And if I get paid for it, all the better for us."

"I know. Since you feel you will never have it for yourself."

Rose shrugged. "I guess that's true. I mean, I know Magdalina wasn't invited to my party, but it's not exactly my fault for the war between the humans and the fairies, is it?"

Theo thought about the Magdust and the fairies who had died as the humans had captured and killed them and the retribution the humans faced. "No, it wasn't your fault."

"It wasn't fair of her to curse me."

"It wasn't fair of them to kill my family, either," Theo agreed.

"When I am Queen of Rhone, we'll find a way to deal with Magdalina and her magic," Rose vowed. "I just need to break the curse she placed on me first."

"Yes." A fierce protectiveness surged through him. How the world would change without Rose in it, he thought. How much his own world would change. Despite the fatigue of the journey, a renewed sense of determination wormed its way through Theo. He sighed.

"What's wrong?"

"Nothing, or maybe everything. I've decided you're right, so you win this time. We need to get down to Titania's terrarium and find a way to dispel the curse on you."

Rose allowed herself a rare moment of hesitation. She thought about how weary their battle finishing off the Eastern Warlord had been, just a few days before, and how tired everyone in the party was, trying to get to the edge of the northern waters of the Aegean. She looked up at Theo, and saw the usual reserves of coolheaded strength, all wrapped up seamlessly in the sharpened angles of his face. He was her rock, the epitome of reason and faith mingled together. She knew he wouldn't have fought for the time off earlier if he hadn't thought it needed.

There was a warm glow that softened in his emerald eyes, as if he could read her thoughts. "It'll be fine, Rosary. There's not one of us that hasn't watched you shoulder someone else's pain these past four years, regardless of your curse or the amount of time you feel you have. And there's not one of us who wouldn't do the same for you, if you will let us."

She snorted and turned away, but his kind words struck her heart and brought a slim layer of grateful tears to her eyes.

"Let's go get Mary and see if Sophia can rig up a makeshift raft for us. If Ethan can get in on it, all the better. For all his map skills he seems to be more of an architect in the making." He stood up and reached down a hand for her.

Her palms felt smooth and strong in his own as he helped her to her feet, allowing Theo to feel the warmth of kinship.

"Okay. I thought I saw a fallen tree down there, by the edge of the forest. Sophia might be able to use that." Rose grinned. "You'll really let me win this time? Even against your better judgment? Despite your unconquerable logic?"

"There's a good reason you're 'Rosary' to me," Theo teased, chuckling a bit, yanking playfully at one of her sun-colored locks. "Go get everyone ready while I say my prayers."

2

“I can't believe we made it.”

At Sophia's cheerful announcement, all of them turned and gave her varying degrees of a glare. Sophia giggled, the bandage bound around her left eye wrinkling as she laughed. The sound echoed throughout the underground cave, causing more of a disparity on Rose and her friends.

“If that's really how you feel, the next time you aren't sure of one of your inventions, give us a warning, will you?” Sophia's younger brother Ethan growled. He pulled his pack out of the remnants of the cavern's tidewater and tentatively began pulling out long scrolls of letters. “I'm going to punch you if your stupid raft ruined my maps.”

“Faith is just as important as skill sometimes,” Sophia reminded him. “And I'll ignore the threat, since we both know first of all, your maps are likely fine, and second, I would win in a fight against you.”

“Theo's been teaching me some tricks,” Ethan muttered darkly.

Sophia stuck her tongue out at him. Before she could offer a counterargument, Rose's faithful hawk, Virtue, interrupted by shaking the water out of his wings.

“Augh!” The two siblings both ducked and Ethan howled as a new layer of moisture hit his exposed map.

“That's enough.” Normally, Rose did not feel the need to interject into one of Sophia and Ethan's squabbles. But now they were safely tucked into the cliffs of northern Greek isles, she needed to take account of what was needed to be done.

"Virtue," she called, holding up her right arm. Instantly, her long-time friend and gyrfalcon came soaring through the darkness of the cave her to her. Rose smiled and stroked him under his beak, gaining a soft coo in response. Virtue had been only one of two bright spots during the fateful night of her seventh birthday—an event otherwise circumvented in conversation and in Rose's memory. Virtue had been given to her by her father, and he had been with her ever since.

Just like the other bright spot, she thought, turning to look at Theo as he hauled the last of the soaking supplies from the cavern entrance.

Virtue cawed softly. "Hey buddy," Rose whispered. "Head up to the others. Ethan, do you have the letter?"

Ethan handed her a small sheet of one of his precious papers. In the shaded light, it was hard to make out his exact features, but the tenderness he had in holding the scroll revealed his disposition. Rose thanked him quietly for the help and he dutifully responded, but he retreated quickly.

I'll have to make it up to him later, she thought to herself, mentally making a note. Ethan did not part from his supplies lightly.

At twelve and thirteen years of age, Ethan and Sophia were the youngest in her crew, and the only ones Rose had largely conscripted. They were not too far from her own age, but still too young to be on their own. But it was better than leaving them to waste away in the family's workhouse, or worse, to be beaten to death by their drunk of a father, Rose thought.

Turning back to Virtue, she tied the letter around his claw, and at her mark, he launched back out into the storm and rain, keeping his flight sure and straight despite the torrid winds and prickly rain. "Fly safe!"

ONCE UPON A PRINCESS

"Do you want me to place a spell on him, so he'll be able to repel the elements?"

Rose grinned as she turned to see Mary fluttering out from underneath Ethan's long, hooded cloak. The small fairy shone out a light all her own, as if it reflected the kindness and uniqueness of her soul. Her red hair, cut short and unevenly on different sides of her face, brightened as she used a handful of her magic to dry off.

"No need, Mary," she said. "Virtue knows his own strength and bravery well, and the odds against him never seem to faze him." Her expression turned speculative. "Besides, we might need more of your power coming up here, to get into the portal."

Ethan returned with a new scroll. "According to the scroll we found, there's supposed to be a tunnel here which leads to the heart of island, and that's where the entrance to Titania's hideaway should be."

"And you're sure we can trust the Eastern Warlords?" Sophia asked. "They didn't seem too bright when it came to fighting."

"That's because a lot of them are scholars, and saw the chance for potential land and knowledge in fighting a war," Rose muttered absently as she looked at the ancient map. "We were lucky we fought them."

"I'm pretty sure they don't feel that way," Theo recalled.

"The Greeks in recent years have been more concerned with art than war," Sophia admitted. "The Warlords no doubt knew this and thought we wouldn't put up a fight."

"Or pay others to put up a fight," Mary chimed in.

"Or that," Sophia agreed. "I guess they were expecting an easy win."

"Easy win or not, a year's worth of fighting is still taxing. But this map is easily worth my weight in gold," Rose said.

"Well, that's fine, but we'll need some actual gold for more supplies on the way back to Rhone," Mary said. "I can't put a spell on all of you and the others, all the time."

"Why can't you just make more gold with your magic?" Ethan asked.

Mary put her hands on her hips as she fluttered over and hovered in Ethan's face. "You obviously haven't been around many fairies in your life."

"I don't think a lot of people have, Mary," Rose reminded her as she laid the map out on a nearby rock. "After all, your family is the only one who still remains friends of the crown of Rhone."

"Well, I suppose. But still," Mary said, turning her attention back to Ethan, "Fairy Magic is not magic to us; it is not learned. We grow with it. It is as natural as breathing is to your kind. But there are rules that go with it, and one of them we have is not to use our power for greed."

"What's the point of having magic if you've got limits on it?" Ethan muttered, inciting a small war as he went back and forth with Mary on the matters of magic and morals.

"Enough," Theo spoke up. "Which way do we go, Princess?"

It always slightly grated her nerves Theo was all proper with her in front of others. She knew he did it out of respect, but it was still jarring.

She pointed to the map and traced a lightened trail. "This is the way," she said. "Mary, take the lead. Ethan and Sophia, stay behind Theo and me."

Down the darkened cavern tunnels they went, with Mary flying consistently ahead of them. With her light to lead the way, Rose found hope bubbling up inside of her for the first time in years.

Even in the dark, Theo could see the excitement in her eyes, and he could feel it in the air; the lightening of her soul resonated with his own.

After several close passages, a broken bridge, and a few stops to double-check the map, the group finally arrived in a small, circular atrium. There was no window to the outer world, but the bright glow of gemstones and phosphorous sparkled against the cavern sky.

"We're here," Rose said, standing in the middle of the room. "This is it. This has to be it."

Ethan and Mary glanced back at the map. Mary squealed with delight. "I see it on the map! The name of the place just appeared, almost like it was … well, I guess it was magic."

"What does it say?" Ethan asked. "I can't read runes."

"It's the Crystal Gate," Mary confirmed. "The Crystal Gate which guards the throne of Titania, Queen of the Fairies." She flew over and placed a hand on the center of the room.

Rose felt the room shift, and she stumbled as power surged through the atmosphere. She reached out to catch herself, but she ended up catching Theo by surprise.

"You okay?" He gripped her arms, steading her.

"Yeah. Sorry."

"No problem."

The rumbling suddenly stopped; Rose looked up to see the stones and light all around were shining with bright light. Pillars of pure crystalline appeared, framing the room. They began to wash the floor with a flood of light, cause it to fade into nothingness.

"Wow," she breathed, as the portal opened up beneath her feet. She smiled up at Theo. "This is amazing."

Theo was about to agree when all of a sudden the sand and stone beneath their feet dissolved. In an instant, all of them plummeted down into the empty hollows of the earth.

Rose felt the scream rise in her throat, but before any sound could escape her, a hard floor flew up to meet her.

"Ouch!" Rose yelped. She looked around to see her companions had all expressed similar sentiments, except for Mary, whose wings wavered gracefully as she took in her surroundings.

Rose briefly took a scouting glance; there were no reasons to suspect she would not be welcome. Mary had told her before the fairies under Titania's rule were not particularly vindictive, unlike those who were under Magdalina's power.

She felt a pressure on her arms and realized Theo still held her. "I'm good," she said, shaking him off as she stood up.

He grunted and stood up beside her. "This place is beautiful," he said. "Makes me think of Heaven."

There were rows of plants and trees, and flowers were everywhere. Great light beams, in all and every color, streamed down, adding magic to every detail. In the distance, Rose heard running water. Was it possible? she thought. A waterfall down here?

A moment later, she decided it was more than possible. Here, down in Titania's terrarium, in her own perfect and private world, it was a type of Eden, before any harm had come upon Paradise. And it was, in Rose's estimation, the ultimate place for fairies to live in peace and fun.

"Can't say I don't agree with you on that one, Theo." Rose looked to see Sophia and Ethan helping each other up. "Mary, what do you think?"

21

"I think this is a dream," Mary said. Gleaming moisture lit up in her eyes as she swirled around. "This place is just glorious!"

"Well, thank you all for your praise," a new voice said. "It'll be nice to have something to brag about to Gloriana. Sisters can be the best of friends and the worst of enemies, especially when it comes to reputation."

Rose turned toward the voice, to see the small form of the Queen of the Fairies herself. Titania smiled. "Of course, you might know of that yourself."

She looked just as Rose had imagined her to be from all the paintings she'd seen of her, with her bright eyes and sparkling movements. But then, she recalled, it had been said Titania was quite proud. She would be the kind of person who only wanted the best of humanity's painters to sketch her delicate features, and with accurate, if not exaggerated, details.

Awkwardly, Rose bowed to the Queen. It was not something she regularly did, but having learned all the motions of proper behavior before her departure from court, it was passable for respectful. "Queen Titania."

"Yes," Titania agreed, while the rest of the others bowed.

From all around, other voices began to frittle softly, excitedly. Titania held up her hand, and silence ensued. "My friends and family welcome you, Princess Aurora of Rhone," she said.

Rose's eyes jerked up, and Theo had to muffle a laugh. If there was one thing the princess hated, it was to be surprised.

"Maybe I should call you Rose, instead?" Titania asked politely enough. She eyed Theo playfully before adding, "Or maybe Rosary?"

Rose felt warmth fly to her face. "Rose is fine," she said, summoning her calm demeanor.

Titania chuckled. "Rose it is," she said. "I have an affinity for flowers, if you can't tell from my home."

"If you know me, you must know why I am here," Rose concluded.

"We're just getting to know each other, Rose," Titania said with a sigh. "I haven't been introduced to your other group members."

Rose felt her mouth drop in involuntary irritation. Titania ignored her as she perused through the line of Rose's loyal compatriots.

"Well, this is a first," Titania purred as she looked at Theo. "I've never had a priest come and visit me. Are you going to try to convert me?"

"I'd promised not to take more time than necessary down here," Theo replied easily. He'd been in enough public alehouses and inns to know when a woman was flirting.

Titania laughed. "Oh my, gorgeous *and* funny. How would you like to stay down here for a while? You can take all the time you need to tell us about the love of God." She touched his arm companionably. "Contrary to what you might think, we are very cognizant of his reality."

"We're not here for that," Rose spoke up. "We're not missionaries."

"My princess has spoken," Theo said. He tugged his arm away from Titania as he added, "But thank you for inviting me. I appreciate it."

Titania pursed her lips. "I can see why you would appreciate a willing audience, given the impudence of your current one," she told Theo, glancing back to Rose. "My offer is open should you ever change your mind."

"Thank you." Theo gave her a brittle smile in return. He might have known when women were flirting, but he also knew how to say no. He was grateful when she just giggled girlishly and moved on.

Rose shot him a frown, and unable to answer for it, Theo looked away.

Mary dazzled the Queen with a quick show of her skill, and Titania, grateful for the display, clapped. "Wonderful! You are indeed a powerful one." She turned back to Rose. "You're right to keep such a creative artist by your side."

"I know," Rose replied. "Mary is the only one of three fairies who remain loyal to the royal family in Rhone; I do not take her friendship or her skills lightly." Mary straightened proudly.

Titania turned her attention to Ethan and Sophia. When she caught sight of Sophia's bandaged eye, she nearly wept. "You have both suffered so," she whispered. "Let me do what I can to help."

Rose and Theo exchanged interested glances as Titania called three other fairies down to her side, and they all pressed their palms against Sophia's missing eye. A *poof!* of magic wafted out from underneath their hands.

Sophia gasped as her bandage fell away. Rose, Theo, Mary, and Ethan all stared.

"Oh, you twit!" One of the fairies muttered. "It was supposed to match her brown eye."

"I thought blue would go better with her hair," another one said.

"I thought we were doing green," the last fairy whimpered. "Green's my favorite color, after all, and I'm the one who has seniority among us."

"It's brilliant," Sophia said, blinking her eyes and staring all around the hidden fairy world. "No matter the color! I can see again!"

"That's awesome," Theo cheered.

"Yes, that's great," Rose agreed, trying to be supportive. Inside, she had to fight off her impatience. Surely, if the Queen of the Fairies could bestow a new eye upon a girl, she could tell Rose how to break her own curse.

She watched as Titania whispered something soft and placed a small peck on Ethan's cheek, before turning back to her.

"Well, Rose, I am finished with the pleasantries," Titania announced. "I assume you want to get down to business?"

Rose nodded. "Yes. If you know who I am, you probably know why I've come."

"You seek answers."

"I only want one," Rose replied. "I've brought gold and gifts along with me, all in exchange for the knowledge of how to break the curse placed upon me by Magdalina."

"I see."

"Magdalina, who commands the realm of fairies surrounding the kingdom of Rhone, my home and future, cursed me when I was younger. She said I would prick my finger on a spindle of a spinning wheel when I was eighteen, and I would die."

Rose nodded to Mary. "And while other fairies before had gifted me with beauty, grace, and song, so that I might marry well and quickly, Mary tried to adjust the cursed spell at the time. She did, making it a deathlike sleep, rather than death itself. She has charged herself my nurse since that time, and vowed to be with me until the end.

"But I can't just let there be an end. Not like that. Ever since I found out the truth, I vowed I would find a way to be free."

Titania nodded. "I see," she repeated. "I have heard tales of you, Lady Princess, you know."

Rose said nothing as she tried to hide her surprise.

Titania continued. "Word has it that once you found out of your destiny, you insisted on getting your way. You rejected the potential suitors your parents had lined up for you to marry at twelve, in hopes an heir for the kingdom would be born before your death. You demanded to be trained as a knight, and learned how to read, not only in your native language but also in the Runes of the ancient Scandinavians, the Latin of the church, and Greek, for the country which owns the world's arts. You set off from Rhone at thirteen, with only your closest friend and a small guard, fighting for adventure and answers and purpose, despite your young years and the certainty of your demise. And you have accomplished many things these last years. You've waged war and made peace between nations."

She glanced at Sophia and Ethan, the former of which was trying hard to pay attention even as her eye's sudden sight astounded her, and the latter of which was gaping at the water nymphs playing in a nearby river. "You've saved lives and given hope to those who had none."

Titania cleared her throat, commanding the full attention of her subjects and guests. "I admire you for such decisions and such results."

"Thank you," Rose said, nodding her head.

Titania flicked her wrist, and a crystal ball appeared in her hand. "I have no need of the gifts you've brought me. I will help you, as you have helped plenty."

"You can help me?" Rose asked. Her heart beat wildly as anticipation burst like a dam through her countenance.

26

Titania washed her hand over the small crystal, and Magdalina appeared inside of it. Her black apparel, the deadly force of her staff, and the crowning tyranny of her atora all pierced through Rose's heart. Anger, hatred, and even a sliver of pity for the sorceress flashed through her.

"Here she is," Titania whispered. "My half-sister, the daughter of Queen Lucia, our mother, and a powerful sorcerer." She sighed. "We have, understandably, never gotten along."

"So you'll help me? You'll tell me how to break her curse?"

Titania sighed. "There are rules to magic."

As Mary gave Ethan a smug kick to the shoulder, Theo stepped forward behind Rose. He didn't like the sound of Titania's voice. One of his ominous warnings shot through him, and though it had been years since his uncle's death, the call of a coming premonition remained potent.

Titania waved away the crystal ball. "There are rules to magic, even for Magdalina. If she put the curse on you, she is the only one who will be able to tell you how to break it."

Rose felt the blood rush from her head. "So, Magdalina is the only one who knows?"

"Yes." Titania's eyes closed in regret.

Theo placed his hand on Rose's shoulder, trying to get her to stay focused. While he knew she would probably later chide him, he also knew he couldn't leave her alone in this. Not after everything they'd gone through to get this far. "What can you do to help us?" he asked.

"I will give you a gift," she said. "Magdalina is not a full fairy, like myself. She is half-human as well. As such, she has her own weaknesses, and you might be able to use that to your advantage. Your sword, please, Rose."

"My sword?"

"Hold out your sword."

Rose pulled out the sword she had tucked into the scabbard at her belt. She held it out proudly, momentarily thanking Sophia for the recent sharpening and cleaning.

Titania waved her hands over it, and magic spurred the hilt to grow metal vines, which laced around the sword's sharp edges, before burning into the blade. The fire faded, and a new sword appeared.

"What happened?" Rose asked.

"This is no longer your sword, but the sword of my great mother, Queen Lucia. She had her flaws as a Queen, but she was a skilled warrior." Titania smirked. "You might recall the story."

Theo surprised Rose by answering for her. "Queen Lucia fell in love with a man, and to show his love, he became the first knight of Rhone."

"There's a bit more to it than that," Titania huffed. "After he became strong enough, thanks to the Magdust he ingested, he wanted Lucia's throne for his own. He placed her in a special genie bottle, hiding her in the dark, away from everyone else and all light."

"I have never heard that part," Theo admitted, stunned by the dark turn of events the legend took.

Titania shrugged diffidently. "Well, you wouldn't have, would you? No one wants to hear their first knight and King managed to murder fairies and capture their Queen."

"That does take away from the Rhonian pride some," Rose agreed, "and paints us as the villains."

"Yes. But you are not your ancestors, and I am not my mother, am I?" Titania asked quietly.

Rose shook her head. "No. I can't change the past. But I can work for the future."

"Yes, you can. And I believe you will be able to use my mother's sword for good," Titania said. She arranged the sword in Rose's hands, making it cross over her heart. "Above all else, my mother sought worthiness. You, Princess Rose, have lived in loneliness, cursed and set apart by a witch's revenge. Yet you have the unfailing loyalty of a gifted fairy, the admiration of young children, and close companionship of a man of God." She looked around at Rose's companions. "I have a feeling my mother would have found you to be worthy.

"My only caution to you would be to watch where you place your love. My mother is trapped now, for all eternity, until she can be freed from her own self-imprisonment first, and then from her genie's bottle, all because she was not careful with her love."

"I'm not worried about that," Rose remarked dismissively. "Loving me would be too painful for anyone to bear. I have chosen not to love anyone. I will especially not fall in love. Ever."

Theo felt the familiar twist of pain inside his chest. He knew how loneliness, even self-imposed, could embitter the heart.

Titania giggled. "Love is something that is chosen and must also choose." She tried to stifle her laughter at the sight of Rose's face. "However, given your record, I would not bet against you. I do not envy Magdalina in that she has made you an enemy."

3

Rose had gone down to bury her fears, only to find it was her hope that died. Time was also playing tricks on her, and she didn't know if it resulted primarily or secondarily from the fairy world.

The return trip to their campsite was both smooth and silent. Or maybe, Rose thought, it was just that way to her. She could hear Theo guiding everyone along, while Mary murmuring her spells along the way, and Sophia was astounded to find her new eye could also see in the dark ("Wow! They really didn't know what to think! This is grand!") Relief to be back in the human world washed over her tepidly along with the sea spray and the moonlight.

"It's late." The words from her lips were harsh, bungled in her throat. They sounded alien to her, but the rest of her crew, with such loyalty and pity on their faces, nodded in agreement and hurried off to camp for the night.

Only Theo stayed behind. "I'll take first guard," he offered.

"You might as well get some rest," Rose told him. "I'm not going to be able to sleep."

"And leave you to all the glory, should Titania and her ilk decide to abduct us again?"

"She didn't seem that interested in keeping us," Rose muttered. "Well, except for you."

Theo shrugged. "Rather like a pet, I imagine," he dismissed. "I have better things to do."

"Like what?" Rose asked. "Waste your life on a fool's journey, under a silly girl's orders?"

ONCE UPON A PRINCESS

"I have never considered saving your life to be the same as wasting mine, Rosary." He came and stood in front of her, the ease of his presence replaced by an unusual heat rather than familiar warmth. Rose had never before been bothered by the six inches he stood taller than her, but all of a sudden the shadow of his strength imposed itself on her.

The cursed beauty of the moonlight revealed the clarity and sharpness of his eyes as she gazed up at him. "What if you did waste your life though? What if?"

"If I have wasted my life, I have wasted it on you. Willingly." He took her by the shoulders. "And you're far from the fool you may feel like tonight. You're allowed to have doubts and fears like the rest of us, and leaders are supposed to make harder decisions. But God knows I have enjoyed every moment of being out here with you. Well, almost every moment."

"Like the time we were captured by the Gaullian forces?"

Theo smiled briefly at the memory. "I was referring to something a little more recently." He nodded down toward the cavern. "The last couple of moments have not been particularly enjoyable. I know you're upset."

"Really?" Rose pushed back and away from him.

"Yes. I am, too."

"I don't want your comfort or your pity," Rose spat. "I'm too angry."

"That doesn't seem fair," Theo countered. "Don't you pity me sometimes?"

"Why would I pity you?" Rose argued. "You don't know when you're going to die. You don't get to be a prize for some prince or just some scapegoat for an entire nation, even one as small as Rhone."

31

"My parents died as a result of the fairy massacres," Theo reminded her. "At least you still have yours."

"Oh, yes, I have my parents, who are so economical in their treatment of me, they only see where I should marry well. I'm placed on display for the nation to come together and unite over my suffering, all while I am deprived of freedom."

"You have freedom," he said. "You might have had to fight for it, but you have it. Here and now."

"I am not free to live as I choose!"

"Neither am I," Theo argued. "I was sent to the church at a young age, and I have been raised there with the expectation I serve there until there is nothing left of me to give."

"You at least have your brother."

"You have a brother, too, and a sister as well," Theo reminded her.

"In name only. They've been largely kept hidden from the rest of the world, and taught in such a manner as to avoid my fate. But you can be open with your grandfather."

"Yes, my mother's father, who holds himself so closely to the love of God he has none to spare for the rest of us. It was only on his honor my uncle managed to convince him to take over raising us." He glared down at her, refusing to step down. "And he only managed to do that because my uncle died right in the middle of the church floor. I watched it happen when I was only seven. You can't tell me you don't pity me for that. Even a spoiled brat like you should be able to sympathize."

Some of the other guards nearby shifted tellingly in the distance. They were watching as the scene unfolded. Rose grumbled to herself. The last thing she needed was everyone to watch as she burst into tears. "Draw your sword," Rose commanded. "You've insulted my honor, so I challenge you!"

Theo complied easily. "I accept," he said, taking his sword out of his scabbard. He held it up high, prepared to do battle.

Rose did not wait for the count to charge. She sped in and unleashed her fury at him, and he met her blow for blow.

Their swords clanked and clanged in tune; over and over again, for how many hours or minutes, he could not say. The metal clashed and rang out as they dodged blows, lashed out attacks, and buckled under defense.

Theo watched as Rose's fury focused and burned, and felt his own lighten into silent laughter as the sunlight peeked out from the horizon's edge. He kept fighting, knowing Rose would only hate him for letting him bait her into battle.

For some time, they exchanged taunts and insults, curses and threats. Before long, Rose was calm and exhausted, while Theo was drained but happy.

He felt the tide of the battle turning in his favor. It was only at the sight of approaching riders he wavered.

"Hang on. Look," he said. "Rhonian riders."

Rose turned to see a small company of horsemen riding, carrying the flag of Rhone, with the symbol of her father, King Stefanos I, boldly resting on each of the riders and their horses. "They're from my father."

Theo nodded. "I wonder if something's happened?"

"I doubt it." Rose let her sword go limp. "I'll bet anything they were sent to make me come home."

"What makes you think that?"

"Virtue is able to carry messages just fine, as are other hawks and falcons from the kingdom. Why just send me a summons when they knew I would likely ignore it?"

"Good point. And speaking of good points … " Theo used her momentary distraction to duck down and kick her legs

33

out from under her. She fell down on the ground, and he held his sword to her neck in triumph. "You're mine now."

Rose glared at him. "Cheater," she accused.

He smirked. "Hardly."

The riders sent out a trumpet call as they approached. Seeing Theo's gaze briefly divert, Rose took her opening. She lashed out a kick of her own, hitting his knee. He stumbled, falling as Rose jumped up.

"Sorry," she said unapologetically. "But I can't let my countrymen see me lose to a priest. We'll call it a draw. No prize this time."

Another trumpet blast came, and the riders were upon them.

He smiled to himself. "*Only* this once. Next time, you'll lose to me," he warned. But for the moment, Theo gave in and flagged the riders before he stood up behind Rose.

"My Lady," the leader of the cavalrymen greeted. "I am Captain Locke, of the cavalry of the kingdom of Rhone. We are looking for the direction of Her Highness, Princess Aurora Rosemarie Mohanagan, heir to the throne of Rhone. We were told she was last seen at the town a day's ride from here, west of the sea."

"I am Princess Aurora," Rose responded. She sighed to herself. It was clear, close up, the men could tell who she was; they might have been hesitant at a distance but Rose was well aware of her beauty's reputation. It did not matter if she was fresh from a battle; one look at her face, open to the sun and sea, was all the confirmation the men needed. "What is the message you have for me?"

"We have traveled many weeks," Captain Locke spoke. "We have several messages for you and those in your party."

ONCE UPON A PRINCESS

"Well, give them to me," Rose insisted. "There is no need for formalities now, Captain. We are not in my father's court, and my company wishes to be off before the next year."

"Please, Your Highness," the captain begged. "We have traveled several extra days trying to locate you. I have orders from the King to escort you personally back to Rhone for the people's sake. The war between the fairies and the people has broken out again, bringing human bloodshed to the land."

Theo doubted the older man would be physically able to force Rose back to Rhone, should she object, but he did not want to point that out. That's why the man was going with the emotional appeal, he realized. There was nothing more sacred than a monarch's ability and conscientiousness in keeping the kingdom safe.

"Let me see the letter," Rose said with a sigh. It wasn't that she was despairing of her people's troubles; it was that most of the problems with the fairies seemed to be provoked by the humans. She silently wondered if the Magdust trade had resumed while she was gone. A look over at Theo prompted him to ask that all the other letters be given to him.

Captain Locke handed her the scroll from her father, and the rest went into Theo's arms. Theo watched her initially as she peeled off the wax seal, and began reading through it.

When she just frowned, he turned his attention to the bundle of mail the other riders had handed to him and saw one from Thad. His brother's untidy loops of letters sent a wave of nostalgia and homesickness through him. He heard Rose sigh and decided Thad's letter would have to wait until later.

"What's it say?" he asked. He glanced over her shoulder at the mess of words, and wondered briefly if the King had written the letter himself. Either that, or his scribe would

35

ONCE UPON A PRINCESS

need to retire. The scrawlish writing seemed to shake as he deciphered it.

Rose bit her bottom lip. "He wants me to come home."

"I figured that much out."

"To officially abdicate the throne. Or to get married."

Theo paused. *Maybe we should have waited longer for our battle this morning,* he thought. He certainly felt a second wind coming on. "Well ... which, uh, which one are you thinking of doing?"

Her eyes blazed blue lightning into him. "Neither!" she snapped. She tore up the letter into tiny pieces, ignoring the disproving look from Captain Locke. "I'm not going home." She turned and stalked off, heading towards the edge of the cliffs.

Theo grimaced as he realized he had to take care of the messengers himself now. "Gentlemen," he said. "Please, come and make yourselves comfortable at our camp. It is just over there," he said, pointing to where he could see someone else had started a fire.

As Theo led the way over to the campsite, Sophia caught his eye. Her blue-green eye winked at him, and he nodded to her in reply.

"My Lords," Sophia came out and bowed deeply. "I am Sophia, squire to Her Highness, the Princess. It would be my honor to welcome you on her behalf."

The guards were surprised at the notion their princess had taken on a squire rather than a nurse or a maid but said nothing. Theo chatted with the men as Ethan handed out some of their food and drink rations, watching and waiting for a moment where he could read Thad's letter.

When he finally managed to steal away, he grabbed a bottle of ale and headed away from the crowd. He pulled out Thad's letter and began to read.

Dearest Brother Theophilus,

I hope this letter finds you well, and you are making progress in both your journey to find the fairy world for the princess and in your fighting skills.

I am happy to report my mastery of Greek is near fluent and comparable to my Latin skills. Thank you for sending me those pamphlets from the Greek peninsula. I am going to take my priestly vows soon, and Grand Father —my latest name for Reverend Thorne—is accepting of this, and dare I say proud, even though of course he would never admit to being proud of me. It's not like he can be, considering his youngest daughter was supposed to be a nun rather than marry our father. I have been given access to all the libraries the church has to offer as a result of my training, and I …

Theo smiled as his brother wrote on of his love of learning, the thrills of finding new information and how it fit into the old. Theo knew he wasn't so much different from his brother. Thad just liked reading as much as Theo, but Thad found a passion and pleasure in serving others Theo knew he would never have; in setting off with the princess, Theo had hoped to learn the ways of knighthood, to learn how to first protect and fight, rather than comfort and educate.

His eyes caught the end of Thad's rambling, and he nearly choked.

… found several letters of interest here in the church, and Grand Father does not know or else I would most likely be excommunicated. I

found the letter our Uncle Thom wrote to him. Grand Father had stacked it with some of the other letters he'd received in lieu of confessions over the years. It was rather miraculous I found it (for all the man assures me each soul has value, he never seems to worry overmuch at what their bodies and minds are doing, and he has a generic letter of forgiveness sent out) but after reading it, I must talk with you as soon as possible.

I regret to ask you this, since it has been almost four years since you left, but when are you returning? In addition to this discovery, many things here are happening …

Theo felt his fingers tingle. His uncle's letter. How could he have forgotten? Though it had been over a dozen years ago, he recalled that night clearly. His old curiosity sparked inside of him, as he wondered what the letter had said. Maybe it had a clue to his parents' demise, he thought.

And instantly the door in his heart, the one behind which he had locked all thoughts and dreams of revenge, justice, and truth regarding his family's deaths, burst open and unleashed a tidal force of energy. The prayerful resolution to accept the past and move on shattered, bringing him back to the place and time where his uncle had died before his eyes. The possibility of new information swept over him, intoxicating him.

Thad was right; he had to go back, and soon. Thoughts of leaving the princess and the others stung him, but he had a task of his own to uphold.

Maybe Rose was right about my logic, he thought glumly. Sighing, he turned his attention back to the rest of his brother's letter.

ONCE UPON A PRINCESS

Rumors have been circulating back to Rhone of tales of your adventures. While I do agree with you now it was best for the princess to have left, and indeed for the world, her father is in an outrage—he confesses to me some dreadful things—and he has begun seeking suitors out. This is most likely why the war has escalated, as the fairies are never happy to have any humans in what they have deemed their territory. Magdalina herself has been spotted by some of the travelers. Since the princess' eighteenth birthday comes after this year, that alone gives me enough reason both doubt and believe such rumors ...

Theo crumbled the paper, recalling Titania's words. *Only Magdalina would be able to know how to break the curse.* Rose is not going to like this, he thought. But on the bright side, he consoled himself, he would be able to stay with her, if he could only persuade her to head back to Rhone. And, he decided, it was that thought which would easily carry him through the unpleasant conversation which would soon come.

4

∴

Mary made her way to Rose's side quietly as the cavalrymen dined and relaxed around the campsite. She knew full well their prejudice against her kind, and while her older cousins, Fiona and Juana, kept busy at the royal court, she could not blame the humans for their discomfort. Not entirely, anyway.

"Hi Mary."

Mary shuddered at the sadness in Rose's greeting. "I feel like you'd say the same at my funeral," she replied, coming up and hovering at eye level. "Come on, Rose. Cheer up."

"It's not easy to do that, Mary." Rose shook her head. "It's not like I just have to pull a switch and it will take care of itself."

"I can put a happy spell on you," Mary offered.

"No thanks." Rose sighed. "I appreciate the offer, though."

"I know you don't believe in using magic like that," Mary said slowly, "but there are deeper things than magic which work just as well, and you have all of them at your disposal."

"Like what?"

"Like friendship, for one," Mary asserted. "You need not bear this alone, Rose. Aren't I proof of that?"

Rose gave her friend a small pat on the head. "You're right. Thank you."

"And here comes another one," Mary said, gesturing toward Theo's approaching figure. "I've never seen him back down from a battle, whether it was for you or with you, or even both, as it was earlier, when he'd pushed you into it. Your fighting this morning kept a lot of the guards awake."

ONCE UPON A PRINCESS

Rose frowned. Theo had purposely pushed her into battle? But why?

The answer came right after the question. To help her work out her trouble and frustration.

That scoundrel, she thought. But she smiled a moment later. "I hope they put money down on me."

"Some did," Mary assured her, as they both laughed.

That was how Theo found her—laughing again. He knew it helped; the early days of living in the church were unpleasant days, scars on his memory, only brightened and sharpened by the practical jokes Thad had encouraged him to participate in against their crotchety grandfather.

He smiled, hoping he wouldn't ruin it. "Mind if I join you, ladies?"

"Not at all," Mary said. "In fact, I think I'll leave you with Rose. I'm going to scour the woods for some berries before we head home today." She twinkled her wings and flew off.

"Why would she think we're going back?" Rose snorted.

"Why shouldn't we, Rose?" he asked her. The instant fire in her eyes almost made him flinch. Before she could unleash the verbal fury from her mouth, he cut her off. "Look, there's war escalating, and your father is worried about you and the future of the kingdom. And Thad sent me a letter to let me know there are suitors coming in from the surrounding kingdoms."

"That's why the fairies are attacking?" Rose asked. "Never thought I would say it, but good for the fairies."

"Rose."

She immediately regretted her words. "Sorry, Theo. I don't want to go home. It's horrible. Looking back on it, I don't know how I survived thirteen years in it. Defeating the Eastern Warlords and the Talonian Gypsies and the Gaullian

41

Giants–all of these things were easy in comparison to my stifling childhood. All the dressing up and manners and pampering, all the people bowing down in admiration mixed with pity, not for who I am or what I do, but for what role I play … I'll bet anything they feel better I'm not there, so they don't have to worry about me as a person. They only have to worry about the future as a kingdom."

"And that's exactly why you should go," Theo told her.

"What?" Rose frowned. "That doesn't make sense."

"Let them see you for who you've become without them." Theo began circling her, as he imagined it. "Many of them have heard the stories of your adventures. Let them see it. We have the riches and the reputation among the nations. Otherwise, why would suitors still come, even after you'd rejected them, or even frightened them off?" Theo gave her a teasing grin. "Come on, Rosary. I've never known you to step back from a battle."

"This is not an enemy that I can kill," Rose reminded him. "I have trained with the weapons of knighthood, but they have weapons that cut, slice, and wound, just in their words."

"You've also trained with logic, reason, and observation," Theo said. "You are more than their match with all your experiences."

But what if I'm not? What if I fail? What if you're wrong about me? Then what will you do? Rose closed her eyes, unable to bear the thought of Theo seeing her cry. "If–*if*–we go, we'll get there close to my birthday. And then I'll only have one year left before Magdalina's curse comes to fruition."

"All the more reason to go," he pushed. "Magdalina has been sighted around the kingdom's outskirts." He reached out and put her hand on her arm. "We can see if she'll remove the curse from you."

42

Rose thought about it. "I doubt she'd do that," she said.

Theo pointed to the camp. "Maybe we can do something. We have your reputation for making peace between people, right? Maybe we can strike a deal with her."

"Make peace?" Rose blinked in surprise. "Magdalina has proved she has no interest in peace."

"There has to be something more that she wants. Maybe we can give it to her." Theo shrugged. "We will never know what exactly she does want if we don't try, Rosary," he chided gently.

He knew he was dangerously getting close to wearing her resolve down when she did not say anything against his remark. He pressed on. "If nothing else, would you consider doing it for me?"

"You?" Rose cocked an eyebrow. "Why would I go home for you?"

"Well, I haven't seen Thad in close to four years," he reminded her. "It would be nice to see him again." And talk with him about what he's found out regarding our parents' deaths, he added silently.

There was a long moment between them, as Rose searched his face. It was such a familiar face, she thought, resigned. Theo had been her best friend for many years, besides her ward and confidante. He had given up his home in order to follow her and fight with her. She almost smiled as she saw the small scar on his neck, the one he'd sustained in their first battle, as he'd put his newly learned knight skills to their first full-fledged test. The temptation to reach out and touch it, so close to his pulse, hit her unexpectedly.

Instead, she sighed, slumping her shoulders as she caved into defeat. "All right. We'll return."

43

Theo grinned. He snatched her up by the arms and twirled her around as he laughed. "Thank you."

Rose, despite herself, laughed as well. "I suppose I owe you something, after everything you've done for me," she conceded.

Theo frowned as he put her down. Rose fleetingly wondered if she'd offended him, but he just shrugged. "Well," he said as some of his cheer returned, "at least I kept my promise. I defeated you this round."

"Hey! This wasn't a battle," Rose objected.

Theo tugged playfully at a lock of her hair. "Everything's always a battle with you, Rosary." He turned and headed toward the campsite, calling back, "I'll start getting everyone packed up and ready to go."

Rose watched as he left, her pride scorched. She wondered what was wrong with her before admitting there was probably very little that was right.

5

∗⁚∗

"We need to head west." After a moment scrutinizing one
of his maps, Ethan pointed up toward the rocky highlands.
"Rhone is on the other side of that mountain. The castle
should be just through the rest of the forest."

Further up the line of travelers, comments stirred.

"What did he say?" Mary asked. "We're going to rest?"

"Not quite," Rose told her, pushing her helmet's visor out
of her eyes. "Buck up. We're almost there. Another day and
we'll be there. Half-day, if we finish getting through the forest
tonight."

She looked around to see the familiar forest of her youth.
The tall trees shaded them from the blast of the sun; even
wearing their full armor, it was a comfortable temperature.
The fairies, so far, had allowed them to go through the woods
without trouble while the wild animals and other supernatural
creatures whispered around them. Rose would have thought
it was humorous, if the horses they'd procured did not spook
so easily.

Rose watched the scenery with sudden reverence. Here,
during the daytime, she would take Virtue out for some
hawking and hunting. The happy memories made her wistful.
She regretted sending Virtue on ahead to announce her
arrival, even as she knew he would have hated the necessary
passage by sea.

"Your Highness," one of the guards spoke up. "It is too
near nightfall now. I suggest we rest and head off in the
morning, when it is safe."

45

"Safe from what? The fairies?" Rose scoffed. She held up her new sword, taking a brief moment to admire the elegant design once more. "I doubt they will give us trouble. I've got the sword of Queen Lucia, courtesy of Titania herself."

"That seems to be precisely a good reason for them to attack us, Your Highness," a messenger responded. "We mustn't provoke them."

"Excuse me," Rose snapped back. "Last time I checked, I was the heir to the throne of Rhone, and they live in our kingdom's land, freely. No one has banished them, no one has forced them out. If humans and fairies will live together, we must agree on how to proceed together. We will not attack them, but there is no need to fear them should they attack us."

The men shrank back onto their saddles, indistinctively muttering in a range of agreement.

"Easy," Theo muttered behind her. "Magdalina's ambition is still to be feared."

"Only if it goes unchecked," Rose replied. She watched as the men headed out before them. "Or maybe *especially* if it goes unchecked."

"They are merely being cautious," he said.

"Too cautious of the wrath of the fairies, not cautious enough of me." Rose flicked a stray wisp of hair out of her line of vision. "Ethan? Can you come here with the map?"

"Don't let your anger out because your pride gets trampled, Rose." Theo looked away as he adjusted the reins of his horse's bridle. "I know you're tired. Everyone is. We've been riding non-stop for days now, and out of all of us, Sophia and Ethan were the only ones who were able to avoid getting sick on the ship before that. Please take care to curb your temper."

ONCE UPON A PRINCESS

"You're not my governess," Rose sniffed indignantly as he moved away.

"What is it?" Ethan asked. "Everything okay?"

"We're fine. And if we're not, we'll be fine. Let me see the map for this forest."

Dutifully, he presented her with the map of Rhone he'd found a few days prior in a town they had passed through. He pointed to the southeast corner. "This is where we are right now. We need to … "

Rose nodded noncommittally as Ethan continued to point out different paths available for them to take to Rhone's principal city, Havilah. While Ethan went through the easiest and the quickest paths, her attention turned to the Darkwood Forest.

The Darkwood Forest was home to Magdalina's forces. No human had breached it in many years, and certainly no one from Rhone. Located just inside the northeastern tips of Rhone's borders, it was about three days' journey from Havilah's palace.

Once the matter of succession was settled with her father, she would likely have to venture through the Darkwood Forest. The prospect was not comforting.

"What do you think, Rose?"

Rose blinked. "Huh?" She glanced up to see Ethan watching her.

"I was asking about which path you think would be best," he repeated, "given the various obstacles we would face in the forest."

"Oh. Well," Rose replied, as she regained her composure, "I think it would be best if we–"

"Augh!"

A piercing howl screeched through the sky, followed quickly by small explosions and horses rearing.

"Someone is in trouble." Rose pushed Ethan and his map aside as she flipped her visor down and drew her sword. "Stay here, Ethan. Wait for my usual signal."

"Be careful!" Ethan called after her.

Rose did not respond, only heading out, sword first. The rush of oncoming battle was potent after so many days just traveling. She could only hope it was a legitimate fight, not some kind of joke, or worse, some kind of drunken mistake gone even more wrong.

Rose was not disappointed.

A band of fairies had captured a grand carriage. Fairies danced in glee as they sliced through the horses' ropes and scared them off.

A large, powerful-looking fairy, whom Rose assessed to be the leader, laughed cruelly as he picked off the guards one by one, hitting them with spells or enchantments as they attempted to slice him.

"You think your little sticks are a match for the mighty Everon?" he taunted. The last of the guards stumbled, dropping his sword, as Everon used his magic to slit the ground beneath his feet.

Rose smirked as she ran. She would start with the fairies' leader, she decided. He was so preoccupied with the guard he hadn't noticed anyone else coming from behind.

Everon gave his prey a grisly grin as he called his power to his palm. The furious red glow transformed its shape, changing into a bulky, sharp blade. "I've killed many humans before you," he bragged. "And I'll keep killing them long after you're dead. Do you wish to beg for your life?"

Before the guard could answer, Everon laughed. "It's never changed my mind, but it is always amusing to me."

"Perhaps then, you will enjoy giving it a try!"

Everon turned to see Rose's sword just before it struck him. He doubled over, the blackness of his blood oozing from his shoulder to across his chest. His eyes narrowed, watching the small warrior before him.

As he lay on the ground in pain, Rose ducked and rolled, fighting with his minions, their power easily overcome by the grace and stealth of a well-taught opponent. As all of his followers began to flee, she turned back to face Everon.

She held her sword steady as she stood in front of the fallen guard, protecting him. "Last time I checked, humans were still allowed to enter into this forest," she said. "Take your goons and leave these people be."

"They're not from Rhone," Everon insisted. "They are fair game."

Rose, recalling the coat of arms on the carriage, could agree they were definitely not from the area. "Be that as it may, you do not have the right to attack them, no matter what Magdalina has to say about it. Especially if the King has invited them."

"I do not listen to the whims of the humans," Everon spat. "They are so inconsequential. Magdalina and I were here long before them, and we will be here long after they have passed."

"If they are so inconsequential, there is no need to bother with them." Rose readied her blade for another parry. "And you will not be here if you continue to attack them."

"No human sword can stand against mine," Everon hissed, as he stood up and called his power to his palm again.

49

But before he could lash out, Rose slashed her sword across his power, surprising him. He gaped at her as her sword cut right through, leaving his power to implode upon itself.

His fellow fighters gathered around him, and before they could avenge him, Rose held up her sword to a patch of sunshine. "I wield Queen Lucia's sword of light. You have no power here."

Everon bared his teeth against her, but in a flash of light, he disappeared.

Rose grinned at the power of her sword. Titania had said she was worthy of such a sword, and the sword had come through for her.

"I must thank you. You saved my life."

The guard behind her stood up as she turned around to face him. He pulled off his own visor.

She nearly gasped.

Rose was glad her own visor was still in place; he was undeniably the most handsome man she had ever seen. His intensely hazel eyes peered out at her through thick lashes, while the wind caressed his copper hair. A beard, a shade darker, was sprouting slowly but stubbornly on his cheeks and chin. She took in the rest of him in a quick second; he was tall, but only a few inches taller than her; his shoulders were wide and capable, obviously built for battle and, in later years, consulting on weighty matters. Rose judged him to be between five and ten years older than herself; at least a couple older than Theo, she decided.

Realizing he could tell she was openly staring, she quickly put her sword away. "No thanks needed," she assured him.

"I disagree." The man looked around as only a few of the others began to stir, while the others would never wake again.

50

"All of my guards were overcome, and you were the only person standing between me and certain death."

"Your guards?" Rose asked.

"Oh. Yes." The man reached out an empty hand. "Please, allow me to introduce myself. I am Prince Philippos, from the kingdom of Einish."

Rose shook his hand. "Nice to meet you." She reached up and pulled off her helmet. "Princess Aurora of Rhone."

Shock crossed his face, but Rose would never find out what he was most surprised by—her beauty, skill, name, or how he suddenly had a life-debt to an heir of another nation—as two other figures came barreling through the bushes.

"My Lady!" Sophia panted, shining in her own, recently refurbished armor. Her weapon of choice, a large battle axe, parried with the low-hanging branches of the surrounding trees as she came to a halt.

Rose turned to face the other fighter, not even needing to see him to know it was Theo. "You were a bit late," she greeted him.

He took a moment to look from her to the prince and back again. And then he pushed up his own visor. "You know me, Rosary. I had to say my prayers."

"A priest and his prayers." Rose rolled her eyes before turning back to Sophia. "Sophie, run and get the healer's potions; see if Mary will come to help with the carriage." As Sophia ran off, Rose turned back to the prince.

"I'd heard tales of the exiled princess of Rhone," he said carefully, "but I never expected them to be true."

Rose smirked. "We'll see what's true and what's not. I suppose you headed to the palace as well?"

"Yes."

ONCE UPON A PRINCESS

"Prince Philippos … one of the suitors my father has been calling for, no doubt," Rose surmised.

"Yes. Please call me Philip." His eyes glittered with mirth. "My company and I have been traveling for several days. We had hopes of arriving in time for the princess' seventeenth birthday—your birthday, My Lady."

"Don't worry about the formalities, either, Philip. I saved your life. Call me Rose," she offered.

"Rose—" Theo interrupted her and then stopped.

"What is it, Theo?" she asked, surprised to see he was wearing a steely expression. *Is he sick?*

"Uh, please excuse me. I wish to help the others."

Rose was uncertain about his mood, but knew there was nothing to be done about it. She would have to confront him about it later, she decided. "You're excused," she said.

"Thank you," Theo said brusquely, before he turned and headed over to check the men.

"You might not want to be so informal," Philip told her as Theo walked away. "Some people would be too shocked by it."

"I'd wager that's their own problem, then."

"I didn't think princesses were supposed to place bets on anything," he replied jovially.

She laughed and asked, "Just what do you know about princesses? Weren't you the one who just told me that you didn't think the tales about me were true?"

Philip could not resist a grin of his own. "Well, you have me there, My La—Rose."

6

꞉'꞉

Theo's heart murmured distractedly as he watched as Philip once more burst into laughter. The last day had been even more tiring than the previous parts of their journey back to Rhone, largely due to the prince's company, and for Theo, it was not just because three of his men of arms had been injured by a pack of Magdalina's fairy warriors. Prince Philip had taken over much of Rose's time and conversation–understandable, but not practical.

And not welcome, either, Theo decided. Without Rose's company and conversation, he had been bored to distraction, checking over the prince's men for medical or spiritual needs while Rose had talked directions, paths, and decisions over with the Prince.

Theo's posture remained steady and his gaze focused on the path ahead, as inside his mind, the only comfort came from forcing himself further into his plans for revenge.

He would see Thad as soon as he could, he decided. As they moved closer, Havilah's castle would occasionally peek out from the veil of hills and trees; Thad resided in the chapel next to the castle grounds, so close as to be adjoining.

One of Prince Philip's guards stirred on the horse beside him. "Sire?" his voice called out, in a loud and slurring sound, but it was clear to even Theo, who was not inclined to like the prince on sight as the others had, he was loyal and anxious for his master's wellbeing.

"You can relax, sir," Theo told the fallen guard. "Your Prince is well."

"Thank the heavens," the man muttered, before slumping down in his awkward seating on his horse once more.

Theo almost laughed, but instead, pulled the horse's reins, drawing it closer to his own horse. There was no need to let the poor man fall, Theo decided, even if he had been wary of the guard's master.

He turned back to the front to see Rose looking back at him. She gave him an approving look, which he drank in like life-sustaining water, before she turned away, turning back to Philip.

Rose felt wary enthusiasm growing as she began to see Havilah's prominent castle through the thinning trees. "We're almost there."

"Excited?" Philip asked.

The old music of the city called to her ears. The sound of street performers, sales clerks, and servicemen jumbled together with children's tears and cheers, ladies' chitter-chatting and animals' pitter-pattering. Homey smells of the bakery and the sweetness of the florist all rushed her senses, baptizing her in the essence of the home of her youth.

"A little, I guess," Rose admitted. "I haven't been home in four years."

"Only natural for you to have missed it in that case," Philip agreed as they stepped out of the woods. "Why did you leave? I've heard it said you couldn't stand it here. But it seems pleasant enough."

Rose laughed. "I'll agree it *seems* pleasant enough," she agreed. The lightness of her voice left as she continued. "But the people here, while they are busy and preoccupied with their lives, do little more than pity me, and my parents."

"You don't want their pity."

54

"No. Especially since it seems rooted more in their own sadness for themselves." She mimicked a fretting nursemaid. "'Oh, woe is me, for who will rule our kingdom should there be no heir after the princess?'"

"Pity is an easy emotion," Philip agreed. "But also dangerous. It's pretty easy to manipulate people who feel pity for you."

"I might be a living casualty of the war between my kingdom and Magdalina's loyalties," Rose said, "but my life still has value outside of my crown."

"I feel silly for not believing what I'd heard about you," Philip confessed. "You are obviously pretty resourceful, using the curse to your own advantage, and helping others with it. Though," he observed, "the ones you help are not your people."

They don't deserve it. Rose watched as the people began to notice her and Philip, and their respective crests. Several smiled and waved, while others burst into tears. She kept her eyes on the castle as it loomed ever more closely.

The royal palace was cut from the older traditions of stone and wood, built up majestically, and maintained throughout the years of its use. The intellectual culture at court insisted it was a hundred years or more, while the people nearby only concerned themselves with their rulers if they curtailed liberties.

One of which, Rose thought bitterly, apparently was the right to a surviving heir for the kingdom. And that was the trouble, she knew, of her visit. Her father's command slipped back into her mind.

Come home, Aurora, and marry, or abdicate your right to the kingdom rule.

ONCE UPON A PRINCESS

Rose wondered if the people were giving her father reason to force her hand. She prayed a silent prayer, hoping that was not the case. It was one thing for her to assuage her father's worries; it would be another thing entirely for her to try to calm the fears of the people. Fears which were also her own, as her eighteenth birthday's deadline loomed closer and closer in her vison.

As if in answer, the clanking of the castle drawbridge rumbled as it fell, and trumpets and horns blared, as a thunderous voice fell across the sky: "Princess Aurora of Rhone has returned!"

Huge crowds of people gathered seemingly out of nowhere, crying out happily, expressing welcome, relief, and gratefulness to God for returning their princess to them safely.

And this is why my prayers are useless. Theo would chide her for her faithlessness, Rose thought, but there was a reason she needed him to be the one to believe in the things which angered her.

Why would God, who was said to be good in all forms, allow her to be cursed? Why would he not remove her curse from her, even as she asked and begged to be free from it? Rose turned to look at Theo again, wishing he could be by her side. While his answers to her questions were not enough for her–that was, when he gave them at all–there was something about having him around her that comforted her unspeakably, as though he was proof God, assuming he was real at all, had not completely abandoned her.

Rose was about to call out to him to hurry over to her, but she stopped at the conflicted look on his face. Theo was looking at the adjoining chapel to the side of the palace. He turned his gaze back to her. Rose realized that he was torn between following her or heading to the church, to see his brother and grandfather.

Their eyes locked for a long moment.

"Prince Philippos of Einish!" the thunderous voice announced in welcome.

"Rose?"

Rose jerked her head around. Philip waited expectedly for her to move forward into the castle. She glanced back at Theo, briefly, seeing he had headed out. "I'll be there in a moment," she said. "I need to check in with my crew." Before Philip could reply, she urged her horse on after Theo.

"Theo."

He stilled and turned back to her. "Yes, Your Highness?"

She pursed her lips at the formality. The bitterness it left in her throat wiped away any excitement she had to be home. "Come on, don't do that." Her horse stopped beside him. "Aren't you coming to court with me?"

"You are not the only one to return, Rose," he told her gently, though it sounded like an insult. "I am here to see my brother at the church."

"God will forgive you if you wait a while."

"Are you saying you wouldn't?"

Rose's lips quirked up into a smile.

"I'll be up shortly," he promised. "But I must see my family."

"What if you're not in time to escort me to see the King?" she asked.

His nose wrinkled. "I doubt your father will be ready to see you right away. We made good time. He'll most likely schedule a meeting with you through one of his servants."

"Theo ... " It was most likely the truth, Rose conceded silently. But it still hurt.

57

"Sorry." After a moment, he pulled off one of his gloves and reached underneath the long sleeves of his chainmail. Rose couldn't see what he was doing, but a moment later, he reached his hand out to her. "Here."

Rose felt the smoothness of several stones slip against her palm, allowing herself to grip his hand in hers for a long moment, as if she was drawing out strength from him. She smiled. "Your rosary beads?"

"Yes." He winked. "So you can say *your* prayers." He took the reins of his horse once more. "I'll be there soon. Go check on the others, Rosary."

"I was going to do that," Rose called after him as she watched him head for the church stables.

"Where's he going?" Sophia asked, coming up beside Rose on her own horse. "Should I go after him?"

"You're not going to bail on me too, are you?" Rose asked.

"A squire stays by his master's side. Or *her* master's side," Sophia recited dutifully. "But on the off chance I would make things more uncomfortable for you, I thought to spare you." She paused as many people began to peer at them curiously. "I *am* a foreigner here."

Rose scoffed at the onlookers. "Spare me only the excuses," she instructed. "I'll need you and Ethan and Mary all with me in my quarters when you've finished seeing to the horses and Prince Philip's guards."

Sophia grinned. "Can I visit the castle's forage house?"

"Later," Rose promised with a smile. "After we meet with the King. I'll need to make living arrangements for you and Ethan."

"How long are we staying?"

Rose glanced up at the crowds and the tall towers of her home. "We'll see." She glanced back at the space where Theo's shadow no longer lingered. "But probably too long."

7

Long before the church had become his home, Theo had always found comfort in his family. As he entered the chapel, the home of the kingdom's worship and the conscience of its leaders, he knew instantly his brother, Thaddeus, was close.

He took off his visor and smoothed his hair. The ebony locks were fickle in their formation. Trying to look presentable to God and kingdom proved difficult, but Theo hoped his spirit was contrite enough.

"Well, well. If it isn't Brother Theophilus," the old croaking voice called out, and he turned to see his grandfather, Reverend Thorne, coming out from the confessional.

"Hello, Reverend," Theo greeted, tempted but not foolish enough to title him "Grandfather." Theo was not surprised to see the old man who helped raise him had changed little in the four years he'd been gone. The same sternly pressed frock, the same look of general disapproval, and the same intense stare were all still there. Only more crinkles and wrinkles folded into his loose skin as he furrowed his brow. "I see you've been fighting lately."

"I'm serving as a knight now," Theo said. "Well, not officially, but the princess has taught me well."

"So you've forgotten priesthood, have you?" Reverend Thorne shook his head. "Well, I suppose it was a long shot to raise you right. You must have too much of your father's blood in you. But at least your brother turned out well."

Theo grimaced. "Where is Thad?" he asked. "I'd like to see him. I don't have much time at the moment. Princess Aurora"–the name felt foreign and uncomfortable on his

60

tongue—"has just returned home and has asked me to accompany her to see the King."

"It's for the best you stopped here first," Reverend Thorne muttered. "Thad is in the back library of the church, reading. He is studying for his next catechism. But he will be able to show you where your deacon's frock is located, so you'll look decent for the princess' audience with the King."

"But I was going to go—"

"What?" Reverend Thorne snorted. "As a knight? Don't subject yourself to such a useless cause. While the King holds meetings daily with his guards and the council of knights, it has been many years since the King has come to the church. We are in disrepair, we are dying, and the kingdom is dying, from his neglect. If you want to make a difference, trust me, and go as a priest. You want his respect as a fighter? Well, this will make him fear you, and remind him we are called to serve God first, not kings."

Theo gritted his teeth together, trying not to growl. "I'll think about it," he grumbled. "In the meantime, I'm going to see Thad. It was nice seeing you again, Reverend."

His grandfather's face softened only slightly. "No need to lie to me in the house of God, son," he muttered, heading back the way he came. "Off with you."

Theo didn't need to be told twice. He hurried off, down the labyrinthine corridors of the church, looking for his brother.

Theo found Thad right where Reverend Thorne said, in the library. He was hunched over a desk, looking at several layers of books and manuscripts.

"Studying for pleasure or priesthood?" Theo called out.

Thad's gaze jerked up. "Brother!" he cried out, happily. He carefully arranged his papers, and then enthusiastically bounced his way over to embrace his younger brother.

61

Theo was surprised to see Thad had changed as much as the Reverend hadn't. Having spent a good deal of his life looking up to his brother, Theo finally surpassed him in both height and breadth. The priestly robes Thad wore were simple and soft, easily caving under Theo's armored embrace, and his hair was neatly trimmed. His brother's matching green eyes were rested and happy.

"I'm very happy to see you," Thad said, as he drifted out of Theo's returning hug. "You've certainly grown."

"You've grown shorter," Theo teased. "I can see over your head now."

Thad laughed, a heartwarming sound that reminded Theo momentarily of their mother's laugh. "God knows you needed to be taller more than I," he said, "with all the battles you've been fighting of late."

"True," Theo agreed.

"It just means I get the smarts," Thad added smugly.

"Well, I don't know about that … "

The two mocked each other and joked and talked excitedly for long moments, before Theo heard the bells chiming.

"I have to head out soon," Theo said.

"Where are you staying?" Thad asked.

"I was just going to come camp–uh, reside here," Theo said, realizing he would be going without his friends for the first time in months.

Thad pushed on, ignoring Theo's disappointment. "Wonderful. We'll have some time here later to discuss things," he said. "I assume with the celebration of Princess Aurora's birthday, she won't miss you for a few days?"

"I'm not sure if she'll need me around," Theo half-heartedly admitted.

Thad laughed, making Theo's frown deepen. "I'm sorry," Thad apologized, "but unless you've become paranoid, addicted to your knight's work, or your homesickness has already turned to roadsickness, I think it's time you admitted you're in love with her."

Vulnerability sliced through Theo's heart, and he felt visceral rage at his brother's perceptive intrusion on the most hidden secret—and closely guarded fear—of his heart.

"Your silence speaks volumes," Thad observed. "So I was right."

"Why would you think that?" Theo asked in the best neutral tone he could muster. "You haven't seen me, or her, in four years."

"Don't give me a time fallacy, Theo. You're forgetting I've known you your whole life, *and* I was the one who nursed your broken nose after you met her that first time."

"It wasn't broken," Theo huffed.

"Well, broken or not, it was pretty smashed in."

"I deserved it."

"You said as much when you'd met her. You never railed about how a seven-year-old girl could slug you, nor did you, for once, seek to return the favor. Which prompted me, at the time, to worry you believed yourself to be half in love with her already."

"People don't fall in love when they're ten."

"People don't tend to insult their future ruler and live to tell the tale, either."

"Well, I don't really tell that story," Theo muttered. "So let's talk about Uncle Thom's letter. What did it say?"

Any additional teasing Thad would have gladly dispensed to his younger brother disappeared at the change in topic.

"Keep your voice down, would you?" Thad's voice dropped

low for the first time. "The Grand Father doesn't know I've found it."

"Why would he worry about it?"

Thad stilled. "It's not entirely pleasant, for one," he finally said, "and you have to remember, Uncle Thom and Father didn't exactly get along with Mother's family."

"Well, what does he know of love?" Theo asked. "It's not like Mother wanted to go live in the convent over by the coast. She told us before, remember? She fell in love with Father and they got married."

"It's more complicated than that." Thad grimaced. "Father, uh, didn't exactly want to marry her."

Shock made him pause for a moment. "Well, he did, so that's all that matters," Theo said.

"Not quite." Thad reached into his frock and pulled out a faded, folded letter. "It's actually pretty bad."

The yellowed parchment was old, wrinkled and faded in his hands. For a brief second, Theo thought the paper had traces of pink and green patterns.

And then realization hit him, hard. "The Magdust," he said.

If Thad was surprised at Theo's comment, he did not say so; he just nodded. "Yes. From what I know–the Grand Father has mentioned it in some other letters I've read as well–she tricked him into marrying her. Uncle Thom had been out fighting when Father came home from battle–you remember, when he was wounded delivering the message to the King about the Farnish kingdom?–and met Mother, and got married to her. Uncle Thom probably didn't realize until a few years after you were born that something was very off about their marriage."

"I don't really want to hear this, Thad."

"I know," he said, sympathetic. "But take the letter. Read it, and get it back to me. You've always been the one who wanted to make peace with their deaths, not their lives. And you are right; the results aren't going to change because some of the circumstances have."

Outside, Theo could hear the trumpets blasting again. More suitors arriving for the princess' birthday, no doubt, he thought disgruntledly.

"I really will need it back, in case the Grand Father ever does decide to go through his papers again," Thad told him.

"Okay." Theo words were as hollow as he felt. He looked back at Thad. "How did you get through, after learning this?" he asked.

Thad sighed. "You were younger than me, only seven, when our parents were killed and we were taken to the church. I remember some of what Uncle Thom mentions in the letter. And," he added, "I have been here all these years. Marriages are not usually made based on mutual affection, unless it is for the love of money and titles." He dropped his voice down to a whisper. "It would shock you, how many wives and husbands have confessed to me of affairs, prostitution, and illegitimate children."

"Are you cynical, then?" Theo asked. "Is that what you're trying to tell me?"

"Not cynical," Thad replied. "Just used to being sad."

"Is that why you have decided to stick to priesthood?" Theo asked.

"Is the princess the reason you have decided not to?"

Theo didn't take the bait. "I asked you first."

Thad gave a wan smile. "I'll keep trying," he warned. "But for now, my answer to your question is no. I like being here, Theo. I like helping people when they need it; I have brothers and sisters and children here, people who rely on me, look up to me. This place, while you have found it to be stuffy and quiet and boring, is structured and settling to me. This is no last resort for me, as many kings and even our uncle had thought it to be. This is home. I've learned to read and research and write. I need no marriage to look for love or magic, as I've found those here, in God and in books; supernatural love has called me here and bound me to this place, and I have chosen to choose it back, and celebrate it rather than escape it." He paused, nodding to the palace just on the other side of the chapel walls, where Theo knew Rose was getting settled in. "Surely you can understand that. All I long for is here."

"I can understand that," Theo agreed, "even if I have not experienced it yet." His hand reached for the rosary beads he kept around his wrist, only to recall he'd given them to Rose before she left.

The bells chimed again, followed by trumpets blaring, and Thad tugged on Theo's arm. "Why don't I accompany you to the princess? I'd love to see her again."

The wicked playfulness in his smile made Theo grumble, but he hurried after his brother nonetheless, grateful and groaning to be in his company once more.

8

⁓

The maids bustled about in her old room, replacing the curtains to her window, pulling up and shaking out rugs, taking down all the sheets which hung over the furniture, and opening up her closets. She could hear every pronounced "*Tsk, tsk,*" every stifled hum, every muffled curse.

All the rushing around and unpacking made Rose feel even more like a stranger in her home. Not even just a stranger, she thought bitterly, but an unwelcome guest.

Mary laughed next to her, sitting on the edge of a teacup that one of the many faceless maids had brought it only minutes before.

"Are you getting a tea bath?" Rose asked.

Mary giggled. "I was thinking about it. This tea sure tastes good, though."

"I'll take your word for it."

"Come on, cheer up, Rose." Mary gestured around the room. "This isn't so bad, right? When was the last time you slept on a mattress this fine?" Mary flitted over to the bed and jumped on it as if to prove her point. "This is the first mattress I've seen in years that lets me bounce back that wasn't being bounced by a team of horses."

Rose smiled and ran her fingers over the fine silk sheets. "You have a point there," she conceded.

"And Sophia's in the adjoining room over there," Mary said as she pointed to a nearby door, "and Ethan is just down the hall. And of course, my cousins and I are near the throne room." She gave a sly grin. "And Philip's just a few floors below you, if you miss his company that much already."

"Mary!" Rose sputtered. "I don't care about that."

"You seemed to like him well enough. And he's handsome," Mary goaded. "I don't think it would be a hard thing, to marry him and to try to get an heir."

"He's definitely handsome," Rose agreed. "But I don't want to marry someone just to give the kingdom an heir. I could've done that years ago."

"Why didn't you?" Mary asked. "I know it's not ideal. I've given you everything I could, just changing the curse that Magdalina placed on you. But you're running out of time."

"I might be running out of time, but I haven't run out of options," Rose shot back.

Mary cocked an eyebrow. "Is there someone else?" she asked, too innocently for Rose's taste.

"No, of course not!" Seeing the maids glance her way, Rose stood up and turned to the maids. "All right, everyone, thank you. Please get out now."

The maids, all surprised to be stopped mid-task, bowed quietly and retreated out the door. Rose slammed the door behind them, already well aware of their discordant chattering. She turned back to face Mary, ready to denounce all thoughts of any earthly happiness, when she nearly jumped in surprise.

A girl, hardly more an inch shorter than her, stood staring at her from behind the door. With her long black hair, brushed to a bright sheen and hanging free, and her rigid posture, she could have easily passed for eighteen. Her dark eyes stared closely at Rose, examining her as if she was a new species of some sort. Her stare was not quite rude, but not so innocent that Rose missed the playful indignation behind it.

"Where did you come from, Isra?" Rose asked dryly. "Crawling about the tower passages again? The Queen won't like you getting your dress dirty."

The girl frowned at the cold welcome. "It's nice to see you too, Aurora," Isra said. "Nearly four years have passed, and you haven't returned any of my letters."

"I felt obliged to let you rot away in your perfect world, here at home," Rose replied. "My letters would have disrupted you from your studies."

"You really did not think your sister would have wanted you to write, especially after all the long treatises and the epic poems I wrote?" Isra's eyes went wide with an injured quality while Rose tried not to grimace at the thought of the many rolls of letters from Isra she had never read. "Ronan is hoping to hear of the battle stories when he gets back."

Rose frowned. "Where is our darling brother? Did he finally learn to stop following you into trouble?"

"He's making his rounds throughout the kingdom with a royal guard. It's part of his knight's training."

"Oh. Well, he'll have to wait to hear them later."

"I want to hear them, too."

"You're too young for them."

"I'm not two years younger than you."

"*I'm* too young for some of the battle stories."

Isra's chin came up, delicate and defiant all at once. "Theo didn't seem to think I was too young for them. I've saved all his letters."

"You leave him out of this," Rose snapped, instantly making a mental note to strangle her former squire the next time she saw him. "He wrote to you against my orders."

"We were such good friends before, Rora," Isra said, her voice beseeching her sister to recall the good times, even using her special sister name. "What changed?"

Rose nearly spit out, "I turned thirteen!" but she stopped herself. Her thirteenth birthday was the day the King had decided to try to marry her off to any one of a handful of suitors. After scaring most of them off, and angering the rest enough to leave, she'd decided to leave her home as well, and the burden of her curse became her own. Instead, she put her arm around her younger sister. "Nothing changed, Isra. The world just came crashing in on me, and I refused to let it hurt you."

Tears flecked into her younger sister's eyes. "So you hurt me instead."

Rose blanched.

Before she could say anything, Isra shook herself free from Rose's awkward embrace and erected the wall of pride inside of her once more. "The Mother Queen sent me here to tell you she and the King will see you in precisely an hour, down in the ballroom. They want the rest of the city to see you with their own eyes." She shook her head resentfully, adding, "I can't believe she couldn't just send a servant up here to your tower. Although, I suppose when it comes to you, I essentially *am* a servant to her."

Rose said nothing. Once she had been cursed, her mother and father had done everything they could have to help nullify the spell and protect her. The spindles on the spinning wheels were all collected and melted down, and with further taunting, the King ordered all the spinning wheels in the kingdom to be burned. Rose remembered thinking after hearing that, how much he sounded as though he could order the rest of the world's spinning wheels to be burned as well.

70

Finally, after a year of Magdalina's taunting, and unable to secure a way to stop the curse from coming true, the King decided they needed to have another baby. But unlike before, with Rose's birth, they decided to keep it a secret. They had the Queen shut away for weeks, ironically proclaiming a strange sleeping sickness, and a little over a year later, she gave birth to Isra and Ronan, a pair of fraternal twins. The knowledge of their birth was kept hidden, only known to the leaders of the church and the main household of the castle keep.

Because of the secrecy, Isra had grown up in Rose's shadow, watching as people showered her older sister with their love and pity, and in the shadow of the curse, as the King and Queen became more like living martyrs, persecuted and oppressed by the fact their first child's life would be cut short.

Rose could only wonder if Isra felt as used and useless as she did; it was too easy to see Isra was lonely. Isra was also the first member of the royal family to remain ungifted by fairy magic, as King Stefanos had been worried such magic might draw too much attention.

"If it makes you feel better," Rose said, "I've never liked the Crown Princess' tower."

"Why would that make me feel better?" Isra asked, wrinkling her nose.

"You'll get to enjoy it more, should I abdicate the throne and leave it to you."

Isra rolled her eyes. "You won't abdicate of your own accordance," she muttered. "It's been your dream to rule Rhone since we were little and we played make-believe. Remember? You used to make Theo play the King and Ronan would be your son."

"Some things are better off leaving to make-believe," Rose told her, wistful and saddened by the long-ago memories of long-ago hopes and dreams. "Some things only come true in make-believe worlds."

"All the world might as well be make-believe to me," Isra said. "I haven't been out of these walls since you were home last time. You should have taken me with you."

Rose sighed. "If it will make you happy, I will. Someday. I've got to get out of here again soon."

Isra's eyes narrowed in suspicion. "Did someone else tell you?" she asked.

"Tell me what?"

"About tonight."

"What is it?" Rose asked. "I figured it was some kind of tournament going on. I saw the jousting fields being set up."

"The King has decided to introduce me to the kingdom."

Rose raised her eyebrows in angry surprise. "Why? Tell me why," she demanded.

Mary, who had been lounging comfortably in Rose's bed, also shot up. "That's utterly irresponsible of him," she said.

Isra sat down in one of the nearby chairs and picked up the cold teapot. "Mary, since you're up, would you warm this for me, please?" she asked prudently.

Rose nearly knocked the tea out of her hands. "This is serious, Isra. Magdalina could come after you. I would have thought you would be safely wed before the King decided to present you to the kingdom."

"That's silly," Isra said. She flashed an appreciative smile at Mary, who just finished dazzling the teapot with a quick fire spell.

"Silly?" Rose yelled. "Protecting you from a fairy curse is not 'silly.' I would be the one to know!"

"It seems silly to me," Isra retorted. "Why would it really matter? Think about it, Rose. If Magdalina *did* learn about me later, when I have been married and I have children of my own, who is to say she wouldn't go after them? Or even *their* children?"

Rose hated to admit Isra had a point. "I was going to try to make peace," Rose whispered. She sat down in the chair opposite of Isra and put her head in her hands. "This complicates things."

"Make peace? With Magdalina?" Isra burst out laughing. "That's comical. She doesn't want peace. She wants the rest of us to be just as miserable as she is."

"Why is it all the evil people in the world want everyone to be unhappy?" Rose asked, not expecting an answer.

Isra gave her one as lifted the teacup to her lips. "Because it's easier to make everyone else miserable than it is to make yourself happy."

Rose smiled despite herself. "You've grown up while I was gone, didn't you?"

"Not enough so someone would really notice. And no one will, since you've come back." Isra sighed. "Tonight was supposed to be for me. The King didn't actually think you would come home, you know, after you routinely ignored his letters and you either fought off or found a way to escape his guards. He probably thought it would be an easy forfeiture of the crown."

"Our father has never known either of us very well."

"Speaking of which, we should probably go down and see him." Isra set aside her now-empty teacup. "Thanks, Mary."

"No problem," Mary replied with a smile. She suddenly giggled with excitement. "I'm going to get to see Fiona and Juana again!"

"I guess it's just a day for reunions," Rose muttered, putting down her own teacup, still half-full. Looking out at the nearby spiral on top of the church, she fingered the gift Theo had given her. His rosary beads hung from her wrist like a bracelet, but it seemed more like a talisman. She wondered how Theo was doing with his brother, and if he was on his way back to her yet.

9

⁑

As Rose made her way down to the ballroom to meet with her parents, Theo hurried up through the chapel passageways and over the bridge. With his brother at his side, crowds easily parted for the well-known Brother Thaddeus and his strange, but also strangely familiar guard.

A loud bell sang out from the town center nearby.

"It seems the tournament games are starting," Thad remarked.

"I'm glad," Theo said. "I'll want a distraction later tonight."

"Why would you keep fighting?" Thad asked. "You're home. There's no need to worry about food or supplies or money. And you'll always have your reputation to carry to the next one."

"I like to practice." Theo walked through a pair of castle guards into the keep and spotted Rose coming down the stairs to his right. He straightened at the sight of her. "And Rosary likes the distraction."

"Rosary?" Thad asked, ready to tease his brother.

But he instantly recognized Theo's expression and turned to face the woman who had inspired it. Thad found even he had forgotten what a sight the princess was.

"She looks good with short hair," Thad muttered.

"Just don't tell her that," Theo said with a grimace. "Rose hates it when people compliment her beauty."

"After hearing it all her life, I'm sure it's tiresome," Thad agreed. "And beauty is fleeting, compared to what is in the heart and soul."

"That's pretty much how she takes it."

"Still, she's beautiful."

"Shut your mouth; here she comes."

Rose brightened up at Theo's presence. "Theo," she greeted him warmly, as though it had been a year since their parting, rather than the long hours it had really been. She reached out a hand to him before stalling.

"Princess." Theo bowed, thrusting his elbow into Thad's chest. He could hear her sigh, but he caught sight of his rosary beads tied up like a bracelet on her arm.

"Are you ready to go with me to see the King and Queen?"

"Yes. Thad offered to join us as well."

"Excellent." Rose smiled at Theo's older brother. "Theo's missed your company, and there's nothing like having a couple of priests around as witnesses." She wriggled her nose at Theo. "Even one who is not dressed like a priest."

"Especially for a princess dressed up as a knight," he agreed with a grin.

"Theo, is that really you?" Isra stepped forward.

"Isra!" Theo reached out a hand to her as well, taking it and giving her knuckles a friendly caress and a kiss. "You've become quite the lady while I was gone."

"And you've become quite the hero. Thank you for your letters." Isra looked over at Rose, who was clearly not happy she had been interrupted. "I know my sister didn't want you to send them, so I owe you extra thanks."

Rose blushed. "We can reminisce after we meet with our father," she said. "Let's go." She turned to Mary. "Mary, would you go and collect Sophia and Ethan? Please ask them to bring a sample of the treasures we've collected on our journeys. Tell Sophia to wear her sword, and Ethan to bring a small collection of his favorite maps."

"Yes, Rose!" Mary saluted. "I'll return shortly."

"Why all the fuss?" Isra asked.

"It can't hurt to show some of my adventures have been rewarding to the kingdom." Rose shrugged. "Anything to keep them off the topics of marriage or abdication."

The walk to the ballroom took longer than she'd ever remembered or expected. With each step, she felt her heart press against her, climbing steadily into the space between her ears to beat rhythmically with the passage of time.

"We'll be all right, Rosary," Theo whispered, so only she could hear. She gave a shrug and then he added, "By the way, you look beautiful."

Her anger flared, which sparked enough bravery to see her through the last steps into the throne room.

"Princess Aurora of Rhone!" The announcement was declared across the room, but to Rose, it felt like it resounded throughout the world.

She made her way, with her friends and sister flanking her, towards the King and Queen, down the red carpet that went from one end of the majestic room to the other.

The throne room never failed to amaze, she thought, admiring the elegance of the high ceilings and inlaid trim. Even as a small child, she marveled at how it would display her power and rule one day.

King Stefanos I, her father, sat down on the right, having married into the throne. Her mother, Leea, while she was the true monarch by birth, made no secret of the fact she despised politics and left most of the trouble of ruling a nation—even one as small as Rhone—to her husband.

Leea met her daughter's gaze and smiled warmly, glad to have her home; the King, by contrast, frowned, no doubt knowing the difficulty ahead.

"Welcome home, Princess Aurora," King Stefanos announced. "We have long desired to see you again."

She bowed and her party followed suit. As she knelt, she saw Sophia and Ethan, along with Mary and her fairy cousins, walk into the threshold of the throne room. Please let them wait for my signal, Rose silently prayed. The King wouldn't like it if they were interrupted, even if it was because of riches and tales of fame, adventure, or even war.

"Rise," Leea called, standing up. She headed over to Rose and hugged her. "My daughter is home."

The rest of the ballroom attendants erupted in cheers. Trumpets blared and music soared from the orchestra pit below the dancing floor. Banners waved and for the moment, crushed to her mother's bosom, Rose felt her world all but disappear among the many celebratory waves of color and happiness and chaos. She angled herself to see her father smiling on the throne, and felt a wave of relief. He had not moved, but any sign that his heart had was a good sign. After catching his gaze, she gave him a smile. He finally did move, and come over to stand beside his wife, and rumpled her hair affectionately.

Rose squeezed her mother tighter to her, a moment of perfection washing all over her.

And then it was over.

"We'll talk soon, Aurora."

Rose nodded but felt the bile rise in her throat. Was it all an act? she wondered. Or was it possible some affection was real? She wanted it to be real so much, it was too hard to determine if it was or not.

She turned to hug her mother again and caught sight of Isra's expression. Her younger sister, once more shuffled to the side, looked grim.

To her right, she watched as her father headed over to Thad, and shook his hand, whispering something to him as well. Rose wondered what he was telling Thad when the King turned to Theo, and blatantly stared at him with a cold glance. Rose saw a brief flicker of shock before Theo disguised his face.

Something is wrong.

Her mother unleashed her, and Rose looked up at her, trying to read her expression. But her mother had her eyes resting on someone else, and before she could stop herself, Rose turned to see one of the guards meeting her mother's gaze.

It was Roderick, she recognized, one of the four guards her mother had insisted go with her when she'd set out into the world at thirteen. It had been the only condition of her blessing. Rose almost smiled; Roderick had been the one she'd nicknamed "Redbeard," because of his bright ginger hair and shaggy beard. It appeared she should have been paying closer attention when her mother handpicked them for her service.

Anger struck her, making her feel exposed, as she realized she'd had her mother's spy in her midst the whole time.

But as she watched the guard, who was looking back at the Queen, their eyes speaking all the words which were forbidden, she suddenly wondered if he wasn't more than just her mother's spy.

"Mother?" Rose broke the silence between them, too irritated by the tender yearning in her mother's expression.

"Yes, darling?" Leea ran her hand affectionately down Rose's short hair, smoothing it out where the King had ruffled it.

"What's going on?"

79

Leea's eyes turned sad. "We've made you upset."

"A little," Rose admitted. "What's with you and Roderick?"

Leea sputtered. "Nothing," she said. "He's just a dear friend, and he has been writing to me, of course, while you've been out."

"I figured that much out." Rose decided to hold her mother's waywardness against her later, when there weren't so many people shouting and yelling. "What's going on with the throne? And Isra?"

Leea sighed. "You're just like your father, you know. Always wanting to get down to business right away."

"Pleasantries should not be needed between family."

"We are family, but we are in the business of keeping a kingdom," Leea reminded her. "And some of us *like* the pleasantries."

"Well then, how many days of 'pleasantries' am I going to have to put up with before we discuss the King's ultimatum?"

"We thought we would give you till your birthday to discuss everything," Leea mumbled. "It's only a few days away."

Three days suddenly seemed like an eternity. "I could make it to Magdalina's castle in that amount of time," Rose muttered.

"What? What did you say?" Leea asked, distracted once more by the gaze of the redheaded solider. "I didn't hear you."

"Nothing." Rose nearly rolled her eyes before she caught herself. "What are you going to do about Isra?"

"She's our distraction."

Stunned, Rose could only hug her mother once more. "Can I go now?" she asked.

"Pleasantly," the Queen told her. "Go back upstairs and dress for the evening. The tournament has begun, and you'll need to be here every night for the ball."

"Fine. But during the days, my time is my own."

Leea sighed. "You aren't going to embarrass us by participating in the tournament games, are you?"

"I wouldn't dream of embarrassing you." Rose detached herself from her mother, wondering if it would be the last time she hugged her and turned around.

The King had moved on to talk with some of his friends and consulting warriors. He didn't notice as she grabbed Theo and turned toward the door.

"Are we presenting the gifts tonight?" Sophia asked.

"I guess not," Rose told her. "Sorry for making you go through the trouble."

"What about all the stories?" Ethan asked. "Should I begin rounding up some minstrels and singers?"

"What for?"

"To compose songs about your travels." Ethan grinned. "Couldn't hurt to move in and win the people's hearts over."

"Ethan has a point," Theo spoke up. "If you're worried the King is getting pressure from the people, now is the perfect time to quell their fears." Rose exchanged a knowing look with Theo at his words; while she hadn't said it aloud, that was part of what she was worried over.

"We have some awesome stories," Sophia added. "I'll go with Ethan and get them started."

Rose nodded. "All right. Take some coins with you." She turned to Theo. "Come with me."

She led the way through the chaos of the ballroom entrance and the keep's entrance before ducking behind curtain and settling into a hidden corridor. Rose jerked Theo in behind her.

"What is it?" he asked.

"I need you to do me a favor," she said. "Isra told me, and the Queen confirmed it, that they're going to present her as the prize in the tournament, not me."

"Well, that's good, right?" he asked. "So you don't have to worry about pressure to get married. And you know Isra. She'll love the attention."

"This isn't good; this is a disaster!" Rose snapped. "What if Magdalina comes after her?"

Theo thought about it. "Well, they still have Ronan, right? I don't imagine they're going to reveal all their secret heirs. Or else Isra would have been against it even more."

"Stop thinking about Isra." Rose felt the temptation to slap him as she recalled he'd been writing to her while they had been traveling all around, trying to find a way to break her curse.

"I wasn't thinking about her, specifically," Theo objected. "I was trying to think about this from the King's perspective. If Magdalina comes to curse Isra, which she might not—"

"How could she *not* come after my sister?" Rose asked. "She cursed me, didn't she?"

"Well, yes—"

"Well, then, why let Isra go? She wouldn't just ignore her. And I can't let Magdalina curse her." Rose sighed. "I know you wouldn't let it happen, either."

"Of course not." Theo took her hand, momentarily shaking her out of her concern.

Without his gloves on, she could feel all the blisters and calluses of his hands and fingers; but she could also feel an aura of strength and capability as his grip tightened over her own small fingers. She watched as he reached out his other hand and placed it on his other.

"You know I would do anything for you or your sister."

Rose's eyes jumped up to his face, and Theo wasn't sure he should have said anything. Her eyes were wide and her lips were parted in a rare moment of honesty. The darkness of the surrounding passageway suddenly hugged him closer to her as the sudden urge to kiss her crashed through him.

"Rose?" A new voice drifted through the curtain as it was pushed aside.

Rose jumped, pulling her hand free of Theo's, and turned to face the new arrival. "Philip."

Prince Philip shuffled in, his tall figure imposing on the small space they shared. "I saw you come this way and thought I would follow. I didn't realize you were having a meeting with your subordinate."

Theo felt anger boil inside of him, suffocating him.

"We're trying to think of a plan for the tournament," Rose explained. "It turns out Isra is the one who is going to be featured, rather than me."

Philip nodded. "Are you worried about her?"

"Tournaments like this have happened before," Theo said, "where the King might offer his daughter, and the throne, as the prize."

"Sometimes it is not always a tournament," Rose added. "My father was assigned a task, for example." She turned to face Philip. "But I'm worried for Isra. My parents have kept her a secret from Magdalina, and never placed any fairy magic on her. I fear she will become a target for Magdalina as well as the many suitors."

Suddenly Rose frowned. "Did you know about Isra?" she asked Philip.

Philip sighed. "Please don't get upset, Rose," he said. "I knew."

"So you were coming for her?"

"My brother and your father have become close friends," he explained, "as the kingdom of Einish has been attacked by the Grand Isle Kingdom in recent years. The Grandians are determined to capture the isle of my home and kingdom. With your father's help, we have managed to keep them at bay. When we met at the Channel battle, I was introduced and he told me he had two daughters. When the time came to make offers, I would get the first invitation to prove my worth to Rhone." Philip's hazel eyes twinkled in the darkened corridor. "For we all know well how much Rhone concerns itself with worth."

Rose wrinkled her nose. "That's true," she conceded. "Well, then, I will request your assistance as well." Turning back to Theo, she said, "I want you to watch over Isra whenever possible. I don't want Magdalina to get to her, and your priesthood instruction will help. I'm sure my mother has a bunch of duties and formalities lined up for me, so I can't protect her at all times."

Looking over at Philip, she missed the shadow of disappointment as it crossed Theo's face. "Since he'll be with her, you'll have to protect Isra by warning off her suitors."

"I am one," Philip reminded her. "I doubt anyone will take me seriously; they'll only see it as a play for the princess' hand."

"Then *make* them take you seriously," Rose nearly shouted. "I'll not have my sister touted as some grand prize just so her ego can revel in it while our enemy sees her as an avenue of revenge."

She shook her head. "Magdalina has been seen around town. I can't let Isra be cursed as I am."

Philip looked solemn. "One day, when we have time, princess, I have a story to tell you."

"What?" Rose's determination flouted.

"I have a story to tell you," he said, "about myself and who I am. While I am staying at the castle, my crew and I meet at the Golden Fleece Inn following the daily activities. Perhaps one night, you would like to join us?"

Theo frowned. Was Philip trying to woo Rose? he wondered. From the confused look on Rose's face, he could tell she was thinking along similar lines.

"Protect my sister during this tournament, and I will be more than happy to hear your stories later, Philip," Rose replied.

She turned to Theo. With a single look, she said nothing and everything all at once. And then she lowered her eyes and pushed past him. "Now, excuse me. I have my own role to play."

10

⁝⁝

Rose had promised her mother she would do nothing in the tournament to embarrass her family, and she vowed to keep her promise.

By vowing not to lose any of the games she participated in.

"You're not seriously going to joust, are you?" Fiona the Fairy came clucking into the room as Rose was pulling her breastplate over her head.

Rose had to stop herself from telling Fiona to leave her. Out of all the fairies, Fiona tended to be more busybody than body. With her brown hair pulled up into a tight bun streaked with gray, and her long nose and stern expressions, Rose thought of Fiona as a type of mother hen, always trying to manage people or take them under her wing. She didn't always think it was a bad trait, but Fiona seemed to do it out of a desire to control things. And while Mary seemed to genuinely like her, and Juana had a deeply set compassion in her heart, Fiona was always planning plans no one would follow, spreading rumors which had at best doubtful origins, and offering solutions where she "miraculously" turned out to be the hero. That was largely why Rose didn't trust her.

However, it seemed to Rose that her mother the Queen had no such reservations, as Fiona was also her mother's confidante. After the Queen had mandated her presence at the rest of the tournaments nightly balls, Rose felt it best to make sure she had the upper hand when dealing with her.

If nothing else, Rose thought, the last four years had taught her about the necessity of strategy, and the danger of trusting emotions.

"Fiona." Rose forced herself to greet the tiny fairy amiably. "How nice to see you again. Mary and I have missed you."

"I could tell, by all the infrequent letters Virtue came back with. Or should I say without?"

Why is everyone so upset I didn't write? "I'm sure you could tell by the infrequency of the letters themselves how busy we were on the different battlefronts," Rose said as innocently as possible.

Fiona folded her arms across her chest. "Her Majesty sent me here to commend you on your performance in the ballroom last night, not to chitchat about your travels."

"I'm glad Her Majesty was relieved to see I remembered how to dance."

"She also commends you on your special attention to Prince Philip."

"Special attention?"

"You danced with him more than once at the welcome ball, and frequently talked and laughed with him. She is pleased, as is your father, which only makes My Lady happier."

"I met him on the way to castle," Rose explained with a shrug. "He seems nice enough."

And he is handsome and funny. The voice in her head made her sigh. She knew her parents must see Philip as a long-awaited answer to their fervent prayers, but she loathed to see herself do the same.

"I'm sure Isra will make him a lovely wife," she said.

Fiona sputtered. "But, princess, what about you?"

"Haven't you heard, Fiona? On my eighteenth birthday, I'm just going to prick my finger on the spindle of a spinning wheel, and fall into sleeping death."

"But *you* could marry Prince Philip, and secure the crown!" Fiona shook her head in distress. "Dear, dear princess, you need not worry for Isra's sake."

"I don't want to get married, Fiona," Rose told her. "Marriage is for people who have the time to find true love, like my mother and father." She carefully watched Fiona's face as it contorted and her mouth released a snort. She saw her opening and pounced. "I mean, after all, my mother is deeply in love with my father. How could I ever want anything less than what she has?"

Fiona patted her shoulder. "Dear, your mother is not as in love with your father as you would think. He frequently ignores her and leaves her alone while he attends to the matters of the nation. She is a beautiful bride, but he has no interest in attending to her love."

"So ... he loves her but she doesn't love him?" Rose asked, pretending to think this through.

"Well, it's more complicated than that," Fiona told her, "but all relationships are like that."

"So she loves him but he doesn't love her?"

"No, it's not like that. Your mother was offered in exchange for a task, remember?" Fiona asked. "Your mother's father tasked every available man in the nation to search out the Rose Ruby."

"And he found it?"

"Yes, of course. He went on a long journey to the Far East, and there it was. He brought it back, and presented it to the King, and he wed your mother that very day."

"Where's the ruby now?" Rose asked. "I've never seen it."

"Treasures come and go," Fiona muttered noncommittally. "But he loved your mother enough to go and get it."

Either that or he loved the idea of being King. The thought burned through Rose with a clarity as sharp as her broadsword. "And ever since, his love for her has grown cold?" Rose asked.

"Not exactly," Fiona muttered again. "But my point is, affection is not a proper requirement in a marriage for a girl like you or your mother."

"I see," Rose murmured.

Before she could ask about Roderick and the Queen's relationship, Mary and Juana popped into her room.

"My Lady," Juana cried. "I'm so happy to see you again!"

"Hello, Juana." Rose gave her a big smile as she saw the bouquet of flowers in her arms. "Did you miss me so much you brought me flowers?"

Juana giggled. "Oh, I should have thought of that myself, but these are not from me, my lady." She handed the large arrangement of assorted posies to Rose. "These are from Prince Philip. He asked me to send them to you this morning."

"Oh. Well, that was very nice of him."

"It's very sweet," Mary agreed. "First the dancing, and now flowers. He's trying to court you!"

It would take more than amusing company and flowers to break the lock around my heart, Rose thought. She wondered briefly if she hadn't been cursed, would she have allowed herself to get swept up in a romantic daydream?

Hopefully not, Rose decided as she arranged the flowers in a bowl. Curse or no curse, her mother's wandering gaze seemed to be proof a marriage made for reasons of greed and power would not result in a lasting happiness.

What do I want? Rose asked herself silently, as she finished putting on her armor and headed down to the courtyard. She didn't even really know what she wanted, she decided. She'd

89

wanted the crown, if only to prove to others she was not going to die, or fall victim to some curse by a bitter half-fairy. She supposed she just wanted to be free, and that meant she had to be powerful enough to be free.

But there was another wish in her heart, she knew, and she would never let it go, or she would die along with it.

"Rose."

At the sound of Theo's voice, she perked up. "Where's Isra?" she asked him.

"Isra's sitting on the throne by the jousting yard outside," Theo told her, pointing out the window. From what Rose could see, a heavily veiled figure was sitting stylishly between the King and Queen. "They didn't announce it was Isra," he said. "They've only been using her title, 'Princess of Rhone.'"

"So this is a joust for *my* hand?" Rose asked. "Amusing."

"It seems they're playing the tournament game pretty deep," Theo told her, falling behind her as she moved forward. "My guess is they will announce you or her to be the prize, depending on what you decide with your father later."

Rose paused and thought about what Theo said. It was a good guess. "That's probably right," she said. "There's definitely power in being vague. Isra gets all the attention she wants, but she is never in danger. My parents get all the interested suitors to battle and rather than risk their honor, they'll risk my decision to stay and keep the throne or abdicate and succumb to the curse."

"You won't fall victim to the curse if I have anything to say about it," Theo promised.

"Thank you, but we can't worry about it right now. Go to my sister and stay with her."

"I was thinking of fighting," Theo remarked. "If I win, I could ask for my knighthood to be granted, officially."

"Not this time, Theo." Rose met his eyes, surprised to see the depth of the dark circles underneath the green emeralds. "You're the only one who can protect Isra from Magdalina."

"Thad could do it while I participate in the games."

"*I'm* going to fight," Rose told him. "Do you really want to find yourself fighting against me?"

"Scared of me?" he asked her, reaching out to tug a lock of her hair, as he'd done so many times before. Heat flared inside of her again at the affectionate touch, warming her from the end of her hair to the tips of her curling toes.

Yes. Rose quickly shoved that part of her mind aside. "No. But I'm scared for Isra." Her eyes went wide and misty as she added, "Please?"

Theo crumbled inside at her openness, but laughed it off. He'd have to find another way to handle the ache in his heart, he decided. "All right," he told her, before bowing and turning away. "Let me go and get my priestly robes, so your father won't even have to see me."

He was gone before Rose could ask him what he meant. "Thank you!" Rose called after him. She wasn't sure he heard her.

"Rose."

"Huh? Oh, it's you." Rose bowed to Philip politely as she watched Theo's back disappear into the crowds. She turned her face up to see the prince grinning down at her attire.

"I see I'm going to have some steady competition today on the field." Even through his neatly trimmed beard, Rose could see a hint of a dimple.

"I figured I'd help you scare off some of the competition," Rose said.

91

"You might have some luck in keeping the competition from competing," he said, "since no honorable man would willingly joust with a girl, let alone a princess."

"I don't let them see I'm a girl beforehand. I keep my visor down and my helmet on. And I use a different name when I battle."

"I suppose that's allowed," Philip contended. "But I wouldn't want to do you the harm."

"Then you'll let me do the harm to you?" Rose grinned. "I didn't think an honorable man would be given to throwing the match."

Philip's smooth cheeks turned red. "You've quite a wit, Your Highness."

"We'll have to see if it is as sharp as your lance," Rose retuned, already brushing past him to hurry off to the first match of the day. "Remember your promise to me. Look after the princess."

Philip smiled as he watched her speed past him. "I most certainly will."

11

Isra sighed. She felt her eyes closing under the waning midday sun, its heat bearing down on her through her veil. "How much longer?" she asked, turning to her self-appointed guardian. Or, she thought, more likely, her sister-appointed guardian.

"Too long," Theo muttered behind her, before trying to hide a yawn.

She snorted. At least he didn't bother to lie to her. Well, then again, why would he? He was as much her friend as he was Rora's, Isra thought. Or was it Rose now?

The sight of her sister returning after years on the road brought none of the joy she'd had previous to her parting. It seemed like Rora had gone, and Rose had come back. Theo, however, was much more Theo than he had ever been.

She looked at him now. Even in the silly deacon outfit he'd gotten from the church, he looked the perfect mixture of dashing and dangerous. The white frock clashed with his dark hair and sun-washed skin, allowing all the battle scars on his hands, neck, and face to slide more easily into view.

Fortunately, her father, from what she'd seen, didn't look past the priest outfit. "I wonder if Rose looks past it, too."

"What was that?" Theo leaned closer to her as the crowd cheered for the triumphant warrior on the jousting field. "What did you say?"

"Nothing," Isra said. "Any sight of danger to my person?"

"Just expiring from boredom," Theo teased her.

"This is nothing new, you know." Isra sighed. "No one is actually paying attention. Or at least," she said as she slanted

93

him a gaze, "no one worth paying attention to is paying attention to me."

He shrugged. "I'm sure Rose will fix that," he said. "In fact, there she is now."

"*She's* going to joust *here?*" Isra asked. Her lips pouted.

Theo watched with renewed interest in the games as a small armored figure, garbed in familiar colors, headed out onto the field with a horse's bridle in one hand and a lance in another. A rush of pride and admiration involuntarily rushed out from his heart. He knew he would never grow tired of her helmet falling half a head shorter than all the other warriors, or seeing her shoulders square themselves as she went into battle despite her disadvantages.

Isra shot up to her feet. "What if she wins? She can't make an offer for me."

"Well, the joust is only part of the tournament," Theo reminded her. "I think it's safe to say she'll opt out of the last day's trial."

"What is it?" Isra asked. "You never know with Rose."

"Fortunately, in this case, we do know her," Theo replied. "The last day has a singing challenge."

Irsa raised her eyebrows. "Well, that'll do it. I don't think there is anything in the world that would make Rose sing again."

"She's certainly managed to keep that vow as long as I've known her," Theo said with a grimace.

"The day she made that vow was quite comical, as I remember it."

Theo had heard the story from several different sources. On Rose's seventh birthday, the whole kingdom had seemingly turned out in celebration. He knew from later it was at the King's insistence, to show Magdalina her curse could not defeat their spirits.

Rose had always been a gifted musician; the pianoforte, the harp, and even the mandolin had been quickly conquered by her nimble fingers and overflowing love of music despite her youth. It had been said the angels bent near the earth to hear the dulcet tones, and the whole world stilled that it might hear of her voice; Theo did not doubt it, from the way people chatted about it.

When she was asked to sing for her audience at her birthday, Rose complied with a child's willingness to please.

As she began the second verse of her chosen song, she noticed everyone was weeping, and she stopped, finally seeing their sadness for what it was—pity.

She stopped mid-verse, and ran away from the crowds and her parents and everyone else, heading towards the castle chapel.

Only to run into me, Theo remembered, rubbing his nose.

Isra's laugh caught him off guard. "I forgot about that," she said. "That was the day she broke your nose."

"Making it bleed is not the same thing as breaking it," Theo muttered.

"What did you say to her that made her hit you?" Isra asked.

"She asked me why everyone pitied the princess and couldn't stand to look at her without crying."

"So you told her the truth? About the curse and everything?"

"Yes." Theo shrugged. "I didn't know it was her at first; after all, I had yet to see her. That was the first week I'd arrived from the church near my home. But after I told her the story of Magdalina and everything, I told her to stop worrying about it, since it wasn't her problem. And then, after she insulted me, saying I must be blind, since *she* was the princess, I laughed in her face. I told her the princess was supposed to be a model of beauty and kindness, and I didn't think that it was her."

"She wouldn't have liked that." Isra laughed. "No wonder she punched you."

"I didn't say I didn't deserve it. But what I did get out of it is nothing short of a miracle of grace."

"What do you mean?"

"People sometimes ask me why I believe in God," he said softly. "And part of is because of Rose, even if she scoffs at the thought of a holy and divine existence. That day, I insulted her and she punched me. When I got the call to go to the palace the next morning, I was fully expecting to be whipped. After all," he said, looking at her pointedly, "the King had wanted to keep a great many secrets, and I'd managed to spill his biggest one.

"But I learned I was to take my daily lessons with Rose, and I was to be assigned her council in the church. And that's not the most amazing part."

"What is?" Isra asked.

"I got to be her friend." Theo looked on as the horn blared, calling the riders to their posts. "Since then, she gave me her trust, and I have always sought to be worthy of it."

Isra watched as his hand covered the pocket at the side of his frock, where she could see a small scroll had been stuffed inside.

Before she could ask what it was, Theo continued. "And I'll never forget what she's given me, even if we have to say goodbye."

ONCE UPON A PRINCESS

Was he talking about Rose, or himself? Isra wondered. She was about to ask him when a loud *clang!* rang out from the field, and she turned to see Rose had hit her target while dodging the other warrior's lance.

The crowd cheered with wild enthusiasm as the spunky winner did several circles of jubilance. But Isra remained still as she watched Rose peek out her visor, looking up in her direction before her gaze drifted to Theo behind her.

"Do you think you'd win against her?" Isra asked.

"I don't know," Theo admitted. "We're pretty even when we fight. Jousting is about the same, since for all her small size, her speed and aim are hard to combat."

"Are you going to dance with her later?"

"Huh?" Theo frowned as he finally looked back at her. "Dance with her?"

"Yeah. Since you're stuck watching over me all day. You should dance with her later."

"Is there a competition?" he asked.

"Why does there need to be?" Isra asked. "You obviously want to join her."

"I wouldn't mind the fighting," Theo acquiesced. "I could use a distraction to stay awake." He glanced at her with a smile. "Not that you're not interesting to watch, Isra."

Isra laughed. "If I'm exciting to watch while I'm sitting here bored, you must be ill. Especially after all the fighting and traveling you and Rose and everyone did across the world."

"It sounds more interesting with all the exciting parts strewn together," Theo confessed. "I won't lie; it was much more enjoyable than being here. But the food is better here."

"I made Rose promise to take me one day," Isra said.

ONCE UPON A PRINCESS

"I'm not sure how long she is staying this time." Theo looked down to see Philip taking his position on the jousting field. "And she might decide to stay yet."

"I doubt it. She seems to agree with you, that traveling is preferable." Isra hesitated before she continued. "Do you think you'd go off on another adventure and leave her here?"

Theo's hand covered his pocket again, pressing down on the letter he kept safe. He sighed to himself. Isra could be just as irritating as Rose, he thought. Especially when it came to perceiving his own secrets.

"I don't know." He pressed his hands together in front of him, trying to keep them occupied. "I don't really want to think about it."

That was as close to the truth as he could get.

"Okay." Isra sighed and relaxed back into her seat, just in time to watch Philip overcome his jousting adversary.

Theo watched as Philip took off his helmet and waved to Isra from where he stood. As Isra waved back and even smiled–though Theo doubted Philip could see it from the field–he decided to concentrate on his uncle's letter, the one Thad had given him. Otherwise, it was too tempting to worry about any princess falling in love with Prince Philip.

Sir,

My time is short, so forgive this quick note. We have not been introduced due to your objection to the marriage of your daughter Eleanora, but I am the brother of her husband. I regret to inform you of their tragic passing. I have evidence to believe they were killed as a result of their participation in Rhone's forbidden Magdust trading.

As I write this, I am preparing to send your grandchildren to you. As a member of the council of knights under King Stefanos I, I am frequently gone and feel unable to provide for them an adequate home. I beg you to receive them at the church, asking for your charity if not your approval. The boys are innocent and ignorant of their parents' activities. I have been around long enough to know that much. Thaddeus has just turned ten, and Theophilus will be eight in a few short months. I have not confided to them this and plea, as a final request, for you never to tell them. The boys are good-hearted and eager to learn; there is no gain to be had in spoiling their early years with the truth of their mother's transgressions and their father's insatiable greed, nor to tell them of their brutal execution by a dangerous fairy-man called Everon, Magdalina's lead henchman in the war against Rho—

The letter ended in a splatter of blood, well-worn into the parchment after all the years it had been kept safe by Reverend Thorne. Theo supposed Uncle Thom had failed to finish it, as he himself was attacked, probably in his own small house. Or maybe he had followed his parents to a drop-off site, where they had traded the illegal Magdust to strangers, and was caught as he headed to gather Theo and Thad to safety.

There were only two clear memories from what Theo could remember of that night: Uncle Thom dripping with blood, and the pink and green fairy dust patterns glowing in the hearth, as the tapestry, the one his mother proudly displayed in the home of their house, burned into ashes.

No, Theo recalled bitterly, there was another memory: Uncle Thom telling him to forgive his family, and to forgive those who killed them. He felt the raging desire for revenge burning inside of him all over again, as his noble uncle breathed his last, only hoping for the eternal security of his nephew's soul.

ONCE UPON A PRINCESS

It was, out of all of the memories he carried, the one he hated the most.

"Rose is up again. Oh, and look who she's up against. This should be interesting."

Theo jolted back to the present at Isra's words. He looked to see the final round of the joust had started. Rose was taking to the field on one end while Prince Philip pushed down his visor on the other.

"Should I stop her?" Theo asked Isra.

"Could anyone ever stop my sister?" Isra asked, standing up. "I'd better get Mary or Juana ready to go down there."

"You don't think she'll win?" Theo asked.

"Prince Philip hasn't lost a joust yet," Isra told him. "And he's stronger, and pretty fast as well."

Before he could say anything else, the horn blared and the riders were off. Theo watched as Rose took aim, ducked down, and kicked her heels into her horse's flanks. She was determined to win.

Theo's eyes squeezed in pain as their lances collided with their shields. A glaring *clank!* followed by the sound of metal banging onto the hard ground made him look.

Rose was lying on the ground, her armor punched in on the side, with blood oozing out from under her surcoat.

᠅

12

"I'll get him back for it tomorrow at the fencing duels," Rose insisted. "There's no need to baby me about it."

"Forgive me then, as my body does not appear to be able to enact your wishes," Theo muttered back. He held her hands lightly, pulling her gently through the various turns and spins of the dance.

"You could, at least, let me dance with Philip," Rose said. "I'd get him back early, in that case."

"There's nothing I want you to do less," he assured her. "If dancing with me will be the closest thing to resting you do tonight, I'll make you dance with me all night."

"Don't make me hate it."

He gave her a charmingly slanted smile. "You couldn't hate it any more than you do fighting with me."

"But I like fighting with you," Rose argued.

"Exactly. Dancing is just the form our fighting is currently taking."

"After I take down Philip, I'm going to come for you, Theo."

"I suppose I'll have to ask for my rosary beads back then."

"Yes, yes, don't worry. I'll give you plenty of time to say your prayers."

"I'll hold you to that."

"After you picked me up off the field today, I'm sure you'd be able to." Rose followed through a turn, allowing herself a moment to briefly blush. Theo and Isra had run down to see her as some squires and pages had helped her off the field. He'd plucked her up off the ground, not even waiting for her to pull off her armor. She'd felt the deep seriousness of his anger and frustration, all wrapped in concern, as he and Isra had scoured the castle for Mary. As much as her side had hurt from Philip's lance, her heart ached with pleasure as Theo clasped her to his chest.

"Anything to get you to cooperate," Theo said.

She gave him a glittering smile. "What happened to your cold-hearted logic?"

"It's in my other priestly frock."

Rose laughed as Theo twirled her again, and immediately regretted it. Many faces turned at the joyful noise, watching her, wondering about her. Even her father caught her eye.

She merely tried to smile back, but it was for nothing. He narrowed his gaze at her before turning his attention to Theo.

"He doesn't like me," Theo told her as he saw her quizzical expression. "He's probably still angry at me for telling you about Magdalina's curse."

Rose thought about what Fiona had told her about her father and mother and their marriage. "I don't think he's forgiven me, either, for asking."

"Some people do have problems with forgiveness," Theo said noncommittally.

"If you're talking about the situation between Philip and me, I can assure you it'll be fine. He'll gladly apologize by the time I'm finished with him tomorrow."

Theo grinned. "That's not what I was thinking of."

"What were you thinking of?" Rose asked. "Come on, you can tell me."

"I was thinking of my parents, to be honest." Theo didn't want to tell her the whole story. "I talked with Thad some yesterday and, well, was a little surprised to hear my mother had tricked my father into marrying her somehow."

Rose didn't miss a beat. There was no pity, there was no surprise. "My mother was a prize in her marriage," she offered.

"Is that what you fear?" Theo asked. "Being a prize for someone to win?" When she didn't answer, he sighed. "Anyone who loves you, Rosary, will always find you to be a prize. The trick for you would be to find someone who knows he could never be worthy of it."

Theo's quiet tone felt like a condemnation. "I don't know if I agree with that," Rose argued. "Queen Lucia found a way to make her man worthy of her love."

"Yes, but Queen Lucia also lost her freedom. She lost her heart to a man she deemed worthy, but did not respect her in return."

"All the better reason never to do something as foolish as fall in love."

"There are plenty of foolish things to do or not do, regardless of love. I'm pretty sure my mother used Magdust to get my father to marry her."

Rose looked vaguely surprised and deeply curious. "Did she use the enchantment herself, or did she bribe him with the money to be made in dealing?"

"I'm not sure," Theo acknowledged. "Does it matter?"

"If you are asking if it matters to me that your parents had an unhappy or falsely happy marriage, then no. Fiona told me my mother and father are pretty much only on speaking terms."

"People in your mother's position don't really marry for love," Theo reminded her.

"I agree. That's why I don't want to get married. I'll not marry for the sake of the kingdom. I'll only marry for love."

"And yet you don't want to fall in love." Theo pretended to be in deep thought. "Hmm, I can certainly see the logic of that."

Rose nodded in the direction of her mother. "I'm pretty sure my mother is having some kind of affair."

"She wouldn't be the first, monarch or otherwise. Thad was telling me just yesterday there are apparently loads of people running around, being unfaithful."

"That doesn't keep you from getting married, does it?"

He gave her a smile. "I doubt I'll get married."

"Why not? You'd make a good husband," Rose said, surprising even herself at her comment.

"I only want to marry for love, too," he admitted.

"So? You're not cursed like I am. It'd probably be very easy for someone to fall in love with you. Look at Queen Titania. She was practically drooling all over you."

"Thanks." Theo laughed. "But I think I'll stick to mortals. I'd feel weird growing older while my fairy wife would stay young."

They laughed together before he added, "But in all seriousness, I have my own reasons for not wanting to get married. I have some things to do yet, and I wouldn't want to drag a bride or a family into the middle of it."

"Revenge is a sticky mess," Rose agreed with pride.

"And it's about to get stickier," he told her as the dance ended.

Her hands tightened affectionately around his as a new song started. "If you're going to make me dance with you, you're obligated to entertain me. Tell me what else you've learned from Thad."

"I know who killed my parents," he said. "It was one of Magdalina's underlings. Some fairy named Everon. I don't know if he's still out there, or still alive–"

"Oh, he is," Rose interjected. "He was the fairy leading the attack on Philip's caravan."

Theo allowed the information to sink in. "He's still in the woods?" he asked. A heady storm of vengeance brewed deep inside, renewing its hold on him.

"Probably."

"I should go find him."

"Can you wait a few more days?" Rose asked. Her fingers laced themselves around his urgently. "I need you here yet."

Theo sighed. "Must I, Princess?"

What broke her was hearing her title, rather than any name he'd ever had for her; it was as if he was already trying to place some distance between them. She jerked her hands out of his, stopping in the middle of the dance floor. "Never mind. Just go. I know it's important to you, and I have to accept that it's more important to you than I am." She gave him a brittle smile and then turned on her heel and sped toward the nearest exit.

"Wait," he called after her.

He waited until they were clear of the room before he reached out and grabbed her hand. "Rose, that's not fair."

"*I'm* not being fair?" Rose asked.

"No, you're not." Theo maneuvered in front of her quickly, drawing her to the side of the room. "You don't know how long you're going to be here–"

"I have plans–"

"You don't know what you're going to do about your father–"

"He doesn't matter to me–"

"And you have no idea whether or not you'll cave in to marriage in order to keep the throne or not."

"That's not true! Don't you know me at all?"

"Don't you know *me* at all?" Theo asked. "Rose." He reached out, catching her face between his hands. "I honestly don't know, because *you* don't know. You can't deny me my revenge while you deny me your heart."

Rose felt the floor disappear beneath her. "What are you saying?" she asked.

"I'm telling you I've always been here for you. But I can't stand beside you if someone else will, or you decide you want to stand alone." He let her go. "Your father, the King, is making you make a decision. You need to make it. I'll wait for you; I'll stay beside you, as much as I can, for as long as it's my duty to do so. But there are some things that I just can't do."

"It's never been your duty to coddle me," Rose snapped.

"Should I forgo my revenge for you?" he asked.

"No! That's not what I want at all."

"Then tell me what you want!" Theo exclaimed. "Just tell me what you want me to do for you."

"I want you to stay away from me." The words were out of Rose's mouth before she could stop them.

Theo just stared at her, frozen. And then he bowed. "As you wish … Rosary."

Before she could take it all back or reverse the command, he left her. Alone.

106

13

Rose wiped the bleariness from her eyes, silently cursing herself for the hundredth time since she'd woken up. After her argument with Theo, she had tumbled and turned all night in her covers, unable to find peace or any comfort in sleep. Despite Mary's keen work on her jousting injury, the pain in her side made the pain in her heart extra uncomfortable.

Her only comfort at the moment was knowing she was one more battle away from a well-earned nap. She turned with a mocking grin to face her last opponent. "Prince Philip." She gave a graceful bow. *At last.*

"You're not tired, are you, Princess?" Philip asked. "You've already gone several rounds."

"As have you," Rose shot back. "I can more than hold my own against you."

"Do your parents know you've been fighting in the competition?" Philip asked. "I'm just curious," he assured her, seeing the accusing look in her face. "I'm not going to turn you in."

No, he was too kind for that, Rose thought. "No, they don't pay attention to me during the day," Rose told him. "They only care if I embarrass them during the balls."

"Well, bad dancing is considered quite incriminatory in some circles," Philip replied, making her laugh.

"Atrocious," Rose agreed. "Right up there with the rest of the seven deadly sins."

"If we're going to focus on churchly rituals," Philip said, "I feel I should confess to you, I've never fought a woman in battle before."

"That you know of?" Rose asked teasingly.

Philip nodded. "I suppose you're right. That I know of."

"I would have thought the good people of Einish would have appreciated doubling their ranks with the women warriors."

"Our women fight every day," Philip told her. "Maybe not on the battle field with an ax or sword, but they fight every day, taking care of everyone who would cause their own destruction if left up to their own survival. The men and children of Einish all owe it all to the women when it comes to keeping civilization going. I have a high respect for them and all they do."

"I can respect that," Rose agreed.

"Then please let me assure you, I hold you in the same respect; even if I know I will not be worthy of yours." Philip bowed again, before holding his sword up in the starting position.

The battle chime sounded, and the fight began. Rose paced herself, realizing early on that her patience was a key factor in how well she did.

The point of a battle was to be ready to defend primarily; punishment was secondary. Patience was the difference in winning a battle and dominating the enemy, and Rose had enough experience in the past to know patience would pay off in the long run.

Philip lived up to her expectations. He lashed out a moment later, and at once, Rose began to read him as a warrior.

He had a nimble quality to his feet, she noticed, making it hard to follow him at times. But there was a drawback, of course; he was too much of a dancer, too willing to make the battle look good, rather than just win. While she admired him for his artistry, her practicality proved triumphant first. She scored the first point by slicing through his armor at the kneecap.

"Point," he huffed, obviously dismayed at losing a point in the first several minutes.

His strength would be her biggest obstacle. Sizing him up, he was quite tall and his shoulders were broad. But she'd had plenty of practice with Theo, so she wasn't worried about that—

She missed a step and felt Philip's sword slice through the leather of her surcoat. "Point," she conceded. "But you technically missed me."

"I'll try harder next time," Philip promised.

"Hmm," was all her reply was as the battle began again, and she took to analyzing him once more.

After a few more strikes and parries, she resigned herself to a longer battle than she'd expected. Philip was a hard soldier to fight, she decided, because he was handsome. He was strong and svelte, talented and smart; he had the look of a legendary prince fighting off demons, working to protect his lady love.

A resounding *rip!* distracted her from further studying Philip's enchanting fairy-tale face. Rose was surprised; she'd scored the next point by sheer chance. She managed to slice through one of his sleeves as he charged at her; she ducked and rolled away, her sword breaking from her grasp and puncturing the chainmail at his wrist.

One point to go for me. Rose pulled back to settle herself from her unexpected gain. Even good surprises will keep one off balance, Rose recalled.

As Rose and Philip circled each other in a short interim, cheers and jeers came from the surrounding crowds. Several people had bet money on the outcome, while others were there to support their respective knights. Rose caught a glance at Sophia, letting her know she would need her armor tended to once she was done.

"I enjoyed dancing quite a bit with your sister last night," Philip told her. "Isra is very charming."

"She is," Rose agreed.

"She speaks highly of you."

"I'm surprised."

"I'm not." Philip tugged down his ripped sleeve and adjusted his glove. "I am a younger brother myself, and I know well what the adoration of an older sibling feels like."

"Really?" Rose decided to move. She sliced her sword through the air. "What happened to your brother?" she asked. "Why is he not here?"

"He is recently married," Philip told her, trying to angle a successful blow himself. "To a beautiful bride and princess."

"I see."

"It is my hope to have similar success," he continued, paring with her jabs.

"Why? Is she a rich princess as well?"

"No, not really," he told her. "But she loves my brother considerably."

"How do you know that?" Rose asked. "She could have been lying."

Philip's brow furrowed underneath his visor. "You needn't sound so pessimistic, Rose."

"I have to be, being cursed and all."

"She was cursed, too, you know."

"What?" Rose frowned. "Who was cursed?"

"My sister-in-law." Philip dove forward and rolled as Rose pressed forward. "She was placed under a curse by an evil sorcerer. She changed into a swan every day, and it was only by the light of the moon each night she was able to become a human again."

"Really?" Rose faltered, accidentally allowing him an open blow on her; if she had not slipped at just the right second, she would have been hit. "How did her spell get broken?"

"I'd love to tell you the full story when we're finished here."

Rose felt her second wind come flying through her, as her relentless curiosity propelled her onward. "Augh!" she cried out, as she leaped over Philip and grabbed him by the throat, wrapping her sword around him as she pulled up his helmet, just enough to see the barest glimmer of skin.

"I submit," Philip muttered, his voice wavering only in the slightest. "For now."

I won. Rose felt a rush of happiness run through her and she looked up to the crowd. She watched as Sophia cheered for her, and Mary sent off her magical glittering confetti, and Ethan, ever with his coloring pad in hand, held up a poster he'd drawn of her triumph over a nameless warrior, face down in a puddle of blood. Grinning, she looked around for Theo before remembering she'd banished him from her presence.

And then the hollowness slithered in. This is what she had been so worked up about? Soothing her pride? Proving herself to be equal to a man in skill was one thing; finding out she could be as arrogant and conceited as one in victory was another.

Rose lifted her sword from the side of Philip's neck. She stepped back and bowed her head, hiding the disappointment on her face. "You have my respect," she said. "Excuse me."

And then she turned away, put her sword in its scabbard, and headed off before her name could be announced as the winner.

14

Theo expertly skirted around his grandfather's presence as he made his way through the old chapel as he looked for his brother. His brother had never been an early riser, Theo recalled, but then, neither was he. He grimaced as the noon bells rang throughout the small chapel.

By the time he reached the private quarters, the tolls of the bells had diminished into echoes.

He knocked on the door to his brother's small room.

"I'm in the middle of my prayers." Thad's voice called out with just enough of a yawn Theo had to grin.

"It's me."

"Who's me?"

Theo knocked again. "Would you just wake up, Thad? It's me, Theo."

"Oh. All right, hang on one moment." Theo had put his hands over his mouth to keep from laughing as he heard his brother scrambling around, trying to make himself presentable.

"Not shirking your duties as a man of God, are you?" Theo asked.

"Not at all," Thad murmured dryly, opening the door and rubbing the sleep from his eyes. "The psalmist says to make a joyful noise unto our Lord, and before noon, mine happens to be snoring."

"Try telling that to the Grand Father," Theo said with a snicker.

"I'm purposefully avoiding it; he'd think me to too loose with scripture. Hurry up and come in." Thad opened the

ONCE UPON A PRINCESS

door. Theo had to smother another laugh as he saw his brother was wearing his frock inside out.

Theo slid into the room and nearly fell over a pile of books. "Wow, I didn't know Reverend Thorne was starting a new library in your room," he said.

"Yes, yes, laugh it off," Thad muttered. "But how else do you think I'm able to hide things like Uncle Thom's letter?"

"There are more?" Theo asked.

"Of course there are letters of the dying," Thad explained, clearing off a small chair. "But there are also other things of equal interest. I found a manuscript of the old fairy legend of Queen Lucia just last month, for example."

"Queen Lucia?" Theo repeated. "It didn't happen to have the real story of her fate, did it? Titania was pretty adamant that her mother made some horrible decisions."

"I haven't finished reading through it, but it's proving to be interesting," Thad replied. "Magdalina's story is much more captivating at the moment, however."

"Magdalina's story?"

"Yes. Did you know she's only a half-fairy?"

"Titania mentioned something about that."

Thad continued excitedly. "She is the offspring of a powerful sorcerer and Lucia, apparently. The half-mortal blood in her body makes her immune to the weaknesses of fairies, and the half-fairy blood makes her extremely hard to fight against."

"I guess that would explain why she's not as tiny as Mary or the others, too."

"Yes."

Theo thought about it. "How would you defeat her? If she is able to undo fairy magic, and stronger than humans?"

"Are you asking this, or is the princess?" Thad asked.

Theo snorted. "This isn't for her. She's tired of having me around to do things for her. I was just asking because I was curious."

"Curious," Thad repeated. "What happened?"

"That's part of the reason I came to find you," Theo told him. "I read through the letter. Uncle Thom had horrible penmanship."

"Agreed."

"But he said that our parents were killed by Everon, one of Magdalina's minions. Rose said she actually fought with him in the woods. He was the one who attacked Prince Philip's carriage."

"I've noticed they've been getting along quite well," Thad said, running a hand over his chin thoughtfully. "I was at the singing competition part of the tournament last night. I saw her cheer for him after he performed. I heard a rumor she is hoping he'll win."

"That doesn't have anything to do with this," Theo grumbled.

"No, it doesn't, but I was wondering if that was the reason you are upset at her."

"I'm not upset at her for that!" Theo snapped. "She can be friends with whomever she wants to be friends with. And I don't care if she wants Philip to win the tournament. She can marry anyone else she wants, or she can smash anyone else's heart she wants. I don't care."

Thad just looked at him.

Before he could say anything of comfort, Theo shook his head. "She already told Philip and me all she wants is to protect Isra from Magdalina's anger."

"That's why she asked *me* to come to the singing round last night, then," Thad muttered. "I guess that makes sense if she really did banish you from her presence."

"She did not 'banish' me. Not exactly." Theo felt his hands go numb as he clenched them. "Can we go back to Uncle Thom's letter? We're getting off topic here."

Thad clapped his hands together. "All right, brother. Sorry."

"I'm sorry, too," he apologized. "Rose did give me some time off away from her"–that was the least painful way of saying it–"so I have been using that time out in the streets to try to see what I can find out about Everon."

"There would be a lot of gossip going around during the festival for the princess' birthday and the tournament."

"Exactly," Theo agreed. "Which is how I was able to confirm Everon was seen around here lately, and that he has been under Magdalina's command for several decades now."

"He is her son."

Theo went silent with shock.

Thad eyed him curiously. "I told you, I'm reading her story," he reminded him. "And she had a child with a powerful fairy King. She named him Everon." He leaned back against the wall. "Although I suppose by now the Everon we're looking for might possibly have children of his own, so the one the princess fought could be his grandchild or something like that."

"It seems too much of a stretch." Theo drummed his fingers against his knee absentmindedly as he thought it through. "Even though it's still hard to believe Magdalina had children at all."

"Magdalina wasn't born the tyrant she is now," Thad said. "She was actually born with the name Malena. She later changed her name to fit her demeanor."

"Either would be fitting, considering both names come from Mary of Magdala, the woman who housed seven demons within her."

"The observation is sound, and it's good to see you remember the Greek language so well." Thad's tone softened to one of sympathy. "I think Magdalina wanted to take the hope of salvation out of it, especially after the fairy King disposed of her and Everon."

Theo said nothing in reply. Nothing could convince him the woman who cursed Rose deserved his pity, after seeing all the years Rose suffered as a result of her curse.

"The fairies seem to be a fickle lot when it comes to love," Thad continued. "Lucia went through several mates before Benedict."

"Benedict?"

"The man who became the first knight of Rhone. From what I have read, he was one of King Arthur's castoffs."

Theo smiled. "I see why you've been hoarding books. It sounds like you've been enjoying them a lot."

"I do like to read," Thad agreed with a shy laugh.

"Did you find anything about how to break Magdalina's curse?" Theo asked.

"There's only one legend said to be able to break through the spell of any magic," Thad replied. "And that's true love's kiss."

Theo sank into silence again. Rose had decided it would be too painful for anyone to love her many years before. She had set out on her adventures with the same determination she had reserved for keeping herself from falling in love.

ONCE UPON A PRINCESS

Thad caught his brother's expression and quickly added, "But it's not something that's been proven, of course. True love is not always proven with a kiss, and anyway, it seems just a little silly, right? Too easy, maybe?"

"Right," Theo muttered. "Too easy and too hard."

"Especially with all those enchantments about luring people into seductions and all that. I don't think it'll be very helpful to us. Now, if you want to *kill* anyone, I can help you out there," Thad continued, "as there are several proven methods to kill all sorts of creatures in these books."

"Even Everon?" Theo asked.

Thad's expression darkened into a contemplative brood. "Yes, even Everon," he murmured, heading over to one of his pile of books. "Let me just look here … for a moment. I think … I think I have a book which can help us."

It took several moments of Thad thumbing through the various texts and scrolls lying around his room before he plucked one up in triumph. "Ah-ha! Here it is." He handed the scroll to Theo. "Here you go."

Theo squinted at the small handwriting on the ancient paper. "What does it say? I can't read Old Anglo, especially in this small type."

"Right there." Thad pointed to a line of text. "Dragon's blood. There are some dragons with blood that can kill any magical creature." He reached around Theo's shoulder and pulled out a map. Theo caught sight of the faded atlas and, after briefly thinking Ethan would want to see about updating it, noticed it was covered with strange markings.

"What are those?" Theo asked.

"Oh, those. That's the Romani language," Thad explained. "I haven't broken the code of it, but I do know from the pictures here"–he pointed to the small sketches in the map's frame–"that a special cherub guards the deadly dragons."

"Cherub?"

"Yes."

"Like the angel in the scriptures?" Theo asked.

"Yes. Some say she is a lesser cherub, keeping captive the offspring of the deadly serpent from Eden." Thad's eyes glazed over. "I've heard the legend before."

"How do you hear so many pagan legends? You live in a church."

"All truth is God's truth." Thad's eyes twinkled. "And besides, I still enjoy a good pint of mead at the tavern like anyone else, Theo."

"Does the Reverend Thorne, the Grand Father, know of that habit as well?"

"I'm avoiding the conversation with him on it, but only because so much of his holy living is subject to cultural whims." Thad cleared his throat. "You'll have to go with me sometime. There are a lot of travelers who pass through Rhone–many trying to get to the bigger kingdoms around here–and will gladly tell you a tale or two for a pint."

"That's how you heard of the dragons?"

"Yes. The legend says there is a Garden of Thorns, where the dragons live, unable to escape to the other side. Wouldn't that be something to see, Theo?"

"I guess so. If you want to be a dragon kebob."

Thad laughed. "Well, if you look here, the exact location of this map says it is in the Romani territory. It's not too far a journey from here; it would be no more than four months by land, and even shorter if you crossed the sea."

"Certainly no journey is too far to travel for something that can help us kill Everon."

There was a tense silence before Thad spoke up once more. "Are you sure revenge is the best option, brother?"

Theo sighed. "It is the only one I haven't completely tried."

"What of forgiveness?" Thad sat down across from him. "If you haven't forgiven him completely, you can't say revenge is all that's left."

"Enough." Theo stood up. "Everon didn't just kill our parents, Thad; he murdered them. Uncle Thom was mortally wounded by him. And it wasn't just the people in our family we lost, but also our home, even our destinies. Do you really think you would be here, at the royal chapel, if Father had lived?"

"If Father had lived, I might very well be capturing helpless fairies and crushing them into Magdust, much as he did."

Theo sighed. "I didn't mean it like that."

"Why not mean it like that?" Thad asked, his patience wearing thin. "You can't mean we were robbed of a perfect life, or even a normal life. No one automatically gets to have a normal life, Theo. No one is guaranteed *any* quality of life. We are allowed to make of it what we can, that is all."

"I know." Theo's fists churned as he sought to control his temper. "I know, Thad. I'm just upset about it. And I have been for years."

Thad put his arm around his brother. "I know. I get upset to see you this way. I don't want to lose my brother to Everon, too."

"Thad?"

"If I have any advice for you, Theo, it would be to seek to protect those you love, rather than seek to destroy those you hate." Thad sighed. "If you're going to ruin your life, I'd much rather it be for love rather than hate."

ONCE UPON A PRINCESS

15

Theo felt his brother's words haunt him as he left the church. As he headed back towards the castle, anger surged through him, along with doubt and fear and confusion.

Was it really so terrible to know what hate was? Theo wondered. Was it so abysmal to have nothing to live for besides revenge, when nothing seemed to calm the storm inside of him?

Theo was crossing the courtyard when he saw Rose. She caught his gaze and he faltered.

Was it so irrational to believe all the answers to his life's troubles lay at the end of a road filled with thorns and an angelic gatekeeper? Especially when the alternative was to watch his best friend, mentor, and princess pass away into everlasting sleep, loved by her people, used by her family, and possibly tended by a husband who would never know her as he did?

Rose began to move toward him. Theo didn't move.

The road of revenge offered nothing but loneliness, danger, and uncertainty. But surely being lonely was better than being completely helpless.

"Theo." His name on her lips called into his heart, and he wondered for a moment if he was not the one who was cursed, that he had unwittingly bound his heart to a woman who intended only to ignore the power of hers?

"Princess." He bowed respectfully, the motion still strange, yet oddly comfortable.

Rose bit her lip. She'd been unable and unwilling to sleep well the previous night. After her fight with Philip, she knew

121

she needed time alone to sort out what she had to do. And while she had no clear choice or path to pursue when it came to marriage or abdication, she knew she had to apologize to Theo first.

Seeing him struck her; she watched him sauntering around, wondering how he never saw how the other women eyed him with more than a lingering glance. With his strong back straight, and his stride purposeful, only his eyes hinted he was somewhere else. They clouded over in unseen worlds, some that she shared, and others she knew nothing of.

She felt her tongue run dry. Why was it so hard to apologize, to say what needed to be said? Rose wondered. It wasn't like she had been right to treat him like a servant, when he was so much more than that to her.

Cowardice secretly won. "It's about time for my birthday celebration dinner," she said, avoiding the subject. "I was wondering if you would accompany me down to the banquet hall?" Her deep blue eyes settled into his. "Please?"

Theo hesitated.

"I've missed you."

Rose's admission was soft enough Theo was not entirely sure she knew she had said it aloud. After a moment of silence more, a moment of watching her misty eyes, he gave her a teasing smile in return. "You need someone to lead you in prayer, Rosary?"

She giggled before smirking back. "I did wear these strange prayer beads," she said, holding up her wrist, where the gift he had given her jangled cheerfully.

"What do you mean, 'strange?'" he asked, taking her arm and tucking it into his own.

"I've seen rosary beads before. Many of them are plain and the same color or material. You have a lot of different ones," Rose said.

"I'll tell you why, someday, if you'd like."

"Sure." Her eyes lit up. There was something special about the idea of 'someday.' She smiled. "It'd make a good campfire story for when we head out to find Magdalina."

Theo stopped short in his tracks. "*If* we need to find her."

"What are you talking about? Of course we have to go and … " The hall was silent with tense worry as Rose's gaze followed Theo's to the center of the ballroom. Though Rose had no memory of ever seeing her in person, there was no mistaking the towering horns of her atora headdress, the sharp folds of her black robes, and the authoritative rigidness of her staff.

"*Magdalina.*"

Rose pressed her eyes together and blinked, while the rest of the crowded ballroom collectively gasped in horror.

Magdalina turned around as Stefanos and Leea gaped at her. "I see, after all these years, I still managed to turn heads and render crowds speechless." She turned and took a step towards Stefanos. "Maybe I should see about starting a fashion line."

Rose watched her father recover. "Seems like a waste of your talent," Stefanos muttered. "You were always prone to mischief, not helping people."

"And you know well why that is," Magdalina shot back. "Speaking of which, where is your darling sunshine, Princess Aurora?"

Theo dropped Rose's arm and stepped in front of her.

Stefanos cleared his throat. "Haven't you cursed her enough?"

"It was not I who cursed her so much as you have," Magdalina muttered back.

Rose stepped forward, pushing past Theo. "I am here," she announced. Eyeing her enemy warily, she graciously tilted her head. "Welcome to my seventeenth birthday party, Magdalina."

Theo held his breath as Magdalina turned to face Rose. He silently prayed she would be okay; but as he watched the resolution on Rose's face, he was reminded all the time of the fearless boldness of Rose as she negotiated treaties between people and countries.

His breath released itself as peace settled onto him. He knew everything would be okay. Eventually.

"So this is the Princess of Rhone," Magdalina murmured as she came over to stand next to Rose. "Such a pity you cut your hair."

Leea nodded behind her; Rose bit back a sigh.

"But I suppose though it is not the style, it suits you," Magdalina admitted.

"Thank you," Rose said. "And while I don't know what your hair color is at all, I would say you've made your own style as well, with that headdress."

Magdalina was clearly taken aback by Rose's response. Theo stepped up beside Rose, grateful he had decided to wear his knight's armor rather than his priestly frock. His hand rested easily on his sword.

Magdalina was amused at his actions, dismissing him easily in her estimation. Her sneer aimed its venom back at the King. "I see you've raised quite a spirited child."

"My father did little to raise me," Rose said, surprising everyone with her interruption. "And I am no longer a child."

Magdalina looked down at her. "No, I suppose you are not," she conceded, "if you would speak with me as an equal."

"I would," Rose insisted. "Just as I would ask you to remove the curse you placed on me."

Magdalina's sneer curled sharply. "You would speak to me as an equal, but you are far from my equal," she observed. "My mother's sword at your side would confirm that."

"I would ask you to remove the curse as well," Theo spoke up. "I am not your equal, and I well know it, but I also know every sentient creature placed on this earth is capable of mercy."

"Capable of mercy?" Magdalina fumed. She looked at him. "What do *you* know of mercy?" He was about to answer her when she held his eyes, and thoughts of revenge came to mind, revenge over his parents' deaths. "I see you have had seen some religious schooling. I should think you, of all people, would find my curse is rather fitting. That a promised child should suffer for the sake of another's transgression?" She laughed as Theo's gaze dropped to the floor.

"Whose sins should my life atone for?" Rose asked.

"Why, your father's first, and your kingdom's second," Magdalina said. "Wasn't it obvious? Perhaps you are more yet a child than you realize. Indeed, if this is a question of mercy, it is mercy for others, rather than yourself, that prevents any removal of the curse."

Magdalina's eyes darted to the throne, where Mary and Fiona were hovering nervously. "I see it has already been altered. Pity. I would have thought death was more favorable."

"Is there no way you would remove the curse from me then?" Rose's patience was thin.

Magdalina shook her head. "No, I will not. Not after all the trouble I went through. I specifically sealed it with a blood sacrifice," she told Rose, holding out her wrist to show a slim scar.

The Queen moaned and fainted, and Stefanos glared at Magdalina. "Have you come to gloat then?"

"Why, no," Magdalina snarled. "Not at all. I've come to see if you've learned your lesson."

"What lesson?" Stefanos asked. "That your cruelty is too cruel? That for all the times my knights have sought your head, you've only gotten stronger and stealthier? That you would punish me through my daughter for the rise of the Magdust trade?"

"One would think you would be more concerned with your daughter than yourself," Magdalina retorted. "Maybe I am mistaken?" She turned and looked back towards the ballroom entrance. Rose followed her gaze and saw Magdalina's attention fall on Isra, who was accompanied by Philip.

"So what I am supposed to do?" Rose spoke up.

Magdalina turned her attention back to Rose reluctantly. "Well, you have a year left. What do you have to do?" she asked. "You are supposed to be a grown woman. What do you say you have to do?"

Rose felt the unspoken aspects of the question burn into her. *What do you have to do for your father? For your throne? For your kingdom? For anything but your own heart?*

Magdalina nodded, as if reading her thoughts. "I have been watching you, Princess; for all these long years, I have kept watch over you, seen you fight, felt your anger and sadness over your fate." She sneered. "And it is a good curse, too. I should never think to find its equal in all the realms of time. But nevertheless, you have transformed my curse into a blessing in its own right. I suspect," she said, her gaze flicked over to Theo, "there is even more to it than that."

"What are you saying?" Rose asked.

"I'll let you think about it on your own," Magdalina told her, an arrogant smile on her ghoulish face. With one last wicked look at Stefanos, she added, "Happy birthday, Princess Aurora," and disappeared in a flash of grisly, green light.

Rose sighed as the rest of the ballroom was torn between horrified silence and intriguing whispers. "Well, that put a damper on the evening."

16

The imposing nature of the door in front of her seemed to be a grand sort of metaphor. All the knocking over the years before she'd finally left came rushing back, along with the accompanying feelings of anger, neglect, confusion, and frustration. But now, at the moment when she was finally allowed inside, she could not bring herself to enter into its protected realm.

"Are you all right, Rose?" Philip came up from behind her just as she hesitated outside of her father's private council room. "I had just entered the room with Isra when Magdalina appeared."

Rose glanced over Philip's shoulder to see her sister's elegant features entertaining a mask of indifference. "I hope you didn't just leave her to come over here for my sake."

"Oh, no. I don't think I did. I hope I didn't." Philip scratched his head nervously, and Rose almost grinned at his boyishness. From all his manly ruggedness, it was endearing.

"I'm sure she'll forgive you," Rose told him. "But you might want to go see if you can coax it out of her sooner rather than later." She narrowed her gaze in a teasing manner. "Although from your pretty poetry yesterday, I'm sure she'll grant it to you. Eventually."

Philip gave a small smile. "I worry for you at the moment, Rose."

"Worry is not a practical response," she said, wishing she could will away her own worry just as easily.

"What would be, in the face of the unknown and terrifying?"

128

"Prayer," Theo spoke up, as he made his way to stand beside Rose.

"What did you find out?" Rose asked, turning to him.

"Magdalina is nowhere to be found, as we suspected," he said. "Thad is working with the other priests and elders on sealing the castle grounds by anointing them with oil. From all Sophia, Mary, and Ethan could discern, she came by herself, with no backup or guards."

"I know you must be disappointed," Rose murmured, sliding closer to him.

Theo allowed his hand to slip into hers, the familiar gesture of comfort suddenly made unfamiliar by the surprising recklessness inside her.

"It's all right," he whispered back, his breath tickling her neck. He straightened his posture and added in his normal voice, "Sophia and the others wish to accompany you to see your father. As do I."

"May I accompany you as you seek council with your father as well?" Philip asked.

Rose felt a wave of bravery crest over her. "I'm pleased to welcome any and all who would stand by my side during an audience with the King," she replied. "But he might dismiss you."

"You are our leader, Lady," Sophia spoke up, as she came around the corner. "Not even the King could dismiss me."

"That's right," Ethan agreed.

"Ethan and I aren't technically Rhonian, anyway," Sophia playfully reminded her, twisting a lock of her black hair, reminding Rose of her Greek roots.

"I have stood by you during worse days," Theo added. "For worse foes, and with worse weather."

"And I would like the opportunity to pay you back," Philip said, "for the debt of my life, which I owe to you."

"There is no debt," Rose muttered. "Indeed, I am tired of people who only feel attached to me by a sense of duty."

"Then I owe it out of friendship."

"I'd rather have earned it on merit than kindness."

"Kindness is its own merit," Philip said, giving her a wink.

"You have earned the title of our leader, Rose," Mary spoke up, as she led Fiona and Juana to the front of the door. "As well as our loyalty."

A moment passed as Rose looked down the line at her row of friends—a warrior and a priest, a blacksmith and an artist, fairies and humans, new friends and old friends. "Well, then," Rose replied, suddenly only worried her sentiment and her desire to cling to the moment would prevent her from moving forward. "This is the best birthday gift I could have asked for."

Turning, Rose fumbled with the door and forced herself through; no longer only for herself, but for those who would swear their fealty to her.

Stepping through the door, nothing seemed as real as it had when Rose had been dreaming. The walls were bare; the table at which the councilors and the King would discuss politics and campaigns long into the night was in need of repair. Several councilors regarded her from all angles around the table, while others did not seem to be able to look at her at all.

To Rose, the second most disappointing realization was how King Stefanos was the unapproachable father he had always been. The first most disappointing thing was realizing he was the first person who taught her that for anyone, loving her was too painful. Yet she did not, could not, blame him for that.

"Your Majesty," she mumbled, moving forward and bowing respectfully. Her party followed suit behind her.

Stefanos stood up. "Councilors," he called. "You are dismissed. I would speak with my daughter in private."

The councilors in the various chairs stood up and grumbled their compliance, though from their faces on the way out, Rose could tell it was reluctant. *They are worried he'll mess up.*

The thought comforted her.

After the door once more slammed shut, its echo resounding through the hollowness of Rose's stomach, she spoke. "Well, Father, if we are to speak freely, now is the time, at last."

"Aurora," he said, his voice weary and tired, "I'm sure you have a great many questions regarding Magdalina and everything else."

"I do."

"I cannot answer them. I can only say you are answering for them, and that is wrong."

"Yes, it is. You should have enough integrity as a ruler, if not a father, to tell me why Magdalina is punishing you."

"There are some secrets a ruler must take to his grave," Stefanos insisted. "All our great legends have secrets of their own."

"Not all of the secrets should stay hidden," Rose reminded him. "Even Benedict, the knight of our forefathers, is unable to hide from his life's work while he is in his grave."

He sighed. "One secret I will tell you. Your mother and I went many years without having a child."

"I know."

"But our fortune reversed itself; we received word that the God of Heaven had heard our prayers, and was sending us a child. You were a child of promise; you were not a cursed child."

Rose said nothing.

He continued. "We were so happy. So happy. And then, all of a sudden, with her curse, Magdalina stole all our hope and joy away."

"I was still there," Rose reminded him.

"Yes, but the dreams we had for you were not," Stefanos explained. "And so, because of this, I have put this day off as long as I possibly could."

He stood up from his chair at the head of his table, holding up a document scroll in his hand. Stefanos came to a halt in front of her. "Here."

Rose took the paper from her father and looked at it. "My abdication," she muttered, seeing the expectant document. "It looks different from what I'd imagined it would."

"Either that or you can marry a suitor here." Stefanos looked past her to Philip. "I see you've been making friends with some of them."

"And this is what you think is best for me?" Rose asked.

"Not for you, Aurora." Stefanos straightened. "The kingdom. Only you can save the kingdom now."

"What of Isra? Or Ronan?" Rose asked. "They are royal offspring as well. Ronan is the first male-born of the nation in three generations."

"Only you," Stefanos repeated. "You are the heir to the throne. You are the one who is gifted by the fairies, and you were the one prophesized to save the lineage from dying out. Even if Ronan or Isra take the throne, there is danger for them; you saw how Magdalina came in here tonight. There is no stopping her. You can't bring that upon your siblings, can you?"

But you would have me suffer for your own failings? Rose bit back the harsh reply to her father. "So you would have me get married, then?"

"Marriage is not the best option for everyone, Aurora," Stefanos said, sending a rush of mental sympathy to her mother. "But I feel in this case, it is the lesser of two evils."

"So by giving me this scroll," Rose remarked as she thumbed the flimsy parchment, "you are trying to scare me into making a decision? You would have me choose between abdicating the throne, and throwing the kingdom into irrevocable darkness, or you would have me marry, produce an heir, and be chained to someone for the rest of my life?"

"Those are the only options we've been given, Aurora," Stefanos told her. "We have been gracious enough to allow you to select which option. The time has come for you to make it."

Something inside of her broke. Rose furiously ripped up the scroll in her hands. "I choose to make my own destiny."

Stefanos huffed. "What good with that do? You only have a year left before the curse is fulfilled. Magdalina's power is still strong, and she will not remove the curse from you. What can you do?"

"I don't know," Rose admitted. "But I'll not trust my heart to a loveless marriage, nor abandon the kingdom of my blood."

"You already left once," the King reminded her.

"Because it had already abandoned me," Rose objected.

Stefanos sighed. "I need to get your mother in here," he said. "Let me send for her." He turned to Fiona. "Fiona, please send for the Queen." Looking back at Rose, he ordered, "Dismiss everyone else, and we'll have a family meeting."

"No." Rose turned and faced her friends. "These are all people who have stood up in support of me. These are my councilors, Father. I will not dismiss them."

"Dismiss them, please, Aurora. This is a family matter."

"You were the one who assured me earlier it was a kingdom matter. If I am to be a leader in this place, I need to start leading."

"This is outrageous," Stefanos muttered. "Fiona, get me the Queen. Now!"

The tiny fairy disappeared in a flash of light, heading out to fulfill her orders. Rose felt her fury rise up inside.

"*We* are leaving," she announced. "You've had your time with your councilors. I'll take some time and contemplate the options you've given us to consider."

Rose turned to see her friends' reactions vary from shock to determination to approval. She ignored her father as he called her back, and headed out of the room.

Philip approached her as the door shut behind them. "How about we discuss this over drinks?" he asked. "The Golden Fleece Inn has been treating my guards impeccably these last several days."

She had nowhere else to go. Staying at the castle would mean finding herself standing before the King again, and likely sooner than she would like. "Couldn't hurt," Rose agreed. "I could use a more lively setting than this dreadful castle has to offer. Everyone in?"

17

The Golden Fleece Inn was small compared to other pub houses close to the royal grounds, but it was warm and welcoming and bright, even at the late hour Rose and her comrades arrived.

They settled in, momentarily allowing the music and the fun to sweep them along, even as they all knew they had come to talk business. But even Rose, as she was caught up in the atmosphere and tempted by the warm mead, was content to give herself a small break from the dreary circumstances of their venture.

She sat down in a large chair close to the hearth, looking over at her newest confidante. "You never did tell me the whole story of your brother and his wife."

Philip's hazel eyes reflected the warm fireplace blazing inside the tavern as he glanced over at her. He lifted his pint to his lips, taking a quick drink. "I suppose I have yet to tell you the whole story," he agreed.

Sophia came down and sat at Rose's feet with a tankard of her own. "What story?" she asked.

"Careful not to drink the hard liquor," Rose warned her. "I'll need you clearheaded for the night and the morning."

Sophia laughed. "I'm Greek. We can hold our liquor."

Ethan came up behind her with some tea. "Only when you don't drink it," he scoffed.

"Bah, that's not true," Sophia cheerfully denied, giving her younger brother a quick punch to the shoulder as she laughed.

Rose locked eyes with Ethan and signaled him to watch over his sister. He nodded dutifully, but Rose had a feeling he was secretly laughing at her. Sophia was responsible, but she was also tough and stubborn, and thanks to her blacksmithing skills, easily able to wave a hammer around dangerously.

"My brother and his wife are newlyweds," Philip began, his voice rising up and down with the ease of a natural storyteller. "They are happily married and content now, but their courtship was anything but easy or smooth. When he was younger, my mother, the Widow Queen, began scheming to find him a bride after her husband passed. I had just been born earlier that year, and without the King, my mother feared leaving the kingdom in doubt of her ability to rule as much as the continuation of the lineage."

"I can relate," Rose huffed.

"Yes. Being a king or queen is all very well and good, but only if your people are happy and confident in your ability to rule."

"Either that, or they are so poor, so tired, so overworked, and so neglected of a proper education they don't have time to worry about rebellion," Sophia muttered bitterly.

Ethan reached over and put his hand on her shoulder.

"You're right about that," Philip agreed. "But Einish, even though it is a larger kingdom, or perhaps even because of it, has a good system in place. Our local lords and knights all work through their duties, getting checks along the way, and there are more checks to make sure of continuing confidence and integrity within the systems."

"I'm guessing the downside is that it relies a lot on that legacy for the next generations," Theo spoke up. Rose watched as he leaned against the wall, his large hands wrapped around a mug. She briefly smiled at the picture he made, both commanding and inconsequential all at once. It wasn't fair how he did managed such a feat, she thought.

Philip nodded again. "You're right. Our strength has always been our collective agreement on leadership, but without the leadership in place, we are weakened."

"So your mother needed to convince them she was doing the right thing, and your brother would be able to uphold the legacy as well."

"Yes. But we are not so practical all the time in Einish," Philip said. He smiled. "We indeed hold love and compassion among our highest virtues. To help this, my mother, having seen other kingdoms come to celebrate my birth, found that one had not, because the kingdom in question had just celebrated the birth of a princess."

He smiled at Rose. "It was about a year before you were born, if my memory is correct.

"Her name was Juliette, and my brother, Derick, seemed to be a good fit for her. Our kingdoms joined on the far end of our borders, so the idea was to have them meet each summer, in hopes they would fall in love."

Mary, who had settled onto Theo's shoulder, sighed wistfully. "How romantic!"

Philip's mouth curved into a twisted grin. "You would think. Both Juliette and Derick initially hated the idea, and each other as a result. It took them several years to go from being angry to playing angry."

"You said she was cursed?" Rose asked.

"Yes. Before long, a ruthless sorcerer, desperate to gain power, tried to take over Juliette's kingdom. When he failed, he captured her and put a spell on her, trying to get her to agree to marry him."

"Seems a bit unnecessary," Sophia observed.

"Well, I can see the reasons for it," Philip admitted. "The sorcerer, Ruebart, would have needed her support to maintain control over her kingdom. If he had married her against her will, she could have easily pushed for a civil war of sorts."

"A fair reminder that popular people are forces to be reckoned with," Ethan observed, shuttering.

Rose, recalling Ethan's own past, quickly pushed the conversation forward. "You said he put a spell on her?"

"Yes. He placed a curse on her, transforming her into a swan every day. During the night, when the moon came out, she would transform into a human again, so he could pursue her as a potential suitor."

"How did she defeat the curse?" Rose asked.

"Well, Derick, who was finally able to admit to himself—and others—that he was in love with Juliette, began looking for her. When he finally found her, he rejoiced and, with the help of our mother, put together an engagement ball for her, hoping to proclaim his love to the world."

"And his love is what broke the curse?" Rose asked.

"Well, there were some complications along the way, but the curse was broken after Ruebart challenged Derick to a battle, and he lost."

"He lost?" Ethan asked.

"Meaning he died," Philip explained. He took another sip of his drink. "Juliette and Derick were married, the kingdoms were united, and I was sent off to see about finding my own bride." He smothered a chuckle. "I doubt I'll have quite the same level of adventure and suspense in my own story."

"Well, you never know," Sophia quipped. "If you're with us now, that might change some." She smiled. "We've had quite a few adventures before. And Ethan and I have only been with Rose for two years."

"I look forward to it." Philip relaxed back in his chair. "I'm not in any hurry to go back to my kingdom. For the moment, it's safe, and I am not needed, nor am I going to suppose I am missed."

"Why wouldn't you be missed?" Rose asked.

"Because Juliette and Derick are newlyweds, settling in, and all that," Philip said. "My mother has begun to pester them for grandchildren, but the kingdom is still glowing from the wedding celebration. I figure I'll have a few years before another incident must come to help the people maintain good faith in our rule." He frowned. "And there was never too much of my mother's attention left over for me to begin with. When you have a parent trying to run a kingdom, it doesn't allow much time left over for raising a child. Let alone two."

Rose nodded. "Yes, that's true. I'm sure my father just proved that to everyone earlier."

No one said anything in reply. Theo watched the light in Rose's eyes fade as she was no doubt recalling the scene in the castle.

His heart ached for her, and there was only one way he could help. "What do you think we should do about your situation?" he asked. "Anyone have any ideas?"

It was a few moments later when Rose spoke again. "I don't want to get married. And I don't want to abdicate."

"It's pretty easy to name what you don't want," Sophia agreed. "What *do* you want?"

Rose sighed. "Honestly, I want the curse gone. But Magdalina's already said that she wouldn't remove it from me, and Titania told us, she would be the only one who would know how to break it."

"But what if Magdalina is gone?" Ethan asked. "Would the curse be broken then, as it was for Philip's brother and his princess?"

The tavern's lively background music started to swell inside of Rose's heart as she looked at Theo. *Is it possible?*

"I suppose it's plausible," Theo admitted, answering her silent question. "She is only half-fairy. Her mortal blood would have bound the curse to you, and by killing her, it would break the seal."

Philip scratched his head. "I don't see the harm in trying," he agreed. "If nothing else, killing her would prevent her from harming Isra or the other heirs to the kingdom."

"People have been trying to kill her for years," Mary said. "It's not easy."

"But that's because they don't know what we know," Rose replied. "*We* know that she's half-mortal, which makes her immune to fairy magic and still more powerful than other humans." She pulled up her sword. "Lucia's sword should be able to kill her."

"And that wouldn't be all of it, either," Sophia spoke up. "You are unable to die since her curse has to be fulfilled."

"Yes." Rose shot up to her feet. "I don't know why I didn't see it before. If we kill her, the curse would be broken."

"Maybe," Theo cautioned. "*Maybe* it would be broken. We aren't sure it would work."

"But surely there's a way to break the curse," Ethan said. He looked over at Mary. "Isn't that a rule, that all curses can be broken?"

"It's true, but it is complicated," Mary admitted. "You heard Titania. Magdalina is supposed to be the only one who knows how to break it."

"So we kill her to break it?" Theo frowned.

"What else could do it?" Rose asked. "What else could possibly break her curse, Theo?"

Theo recalled what Thad had mentioned earlier. *True love's kiss.* But he avoided her gaze. Between killing a half-fairy and finding Rose an acceptable suitor, he knew he would rather seek out Magdalina's wrath.

Rose began pacing in front of them. "That's it, then." Her mouth was a grim, determined line as she made her decision. "That's our plan."

"What, just go and kill Magdalina?" Mary's eyes were wide. "It's not something that's easily done, Rose. We'd have to go to her castle in the Darkwood Forest, fight her scores of guards, and then we'd have to trap her and prevent her from disappearing on us. And then to kill her, you'd have to make sure she wouldn't survive. Queen Lucia's sword can combat fairy magic, but it is the sword of her mother. Lucia would have been smart enough to place a spell on her sword to keep it from killing her own blood."

"What about something that can kill any magical creature?" Theo asked.

"Like what?" Mary asked. "There are different potions and spells for certain things, sure, but there's nothing that's guaranteed to kill a half-fairy."

"Not even dragon's blood?" he asked quietly.

Mary emitted a small squeak. "How do you know about dragon's blood?" she asked.

"Dragon's blood?" Rose asked, intrigued.

Theo nodded. "It's in a manuscript Thad found in the church's library. It tells of a place in the Romani territory where dragons live, protected and guarded, and their blood can kill any magical creature—especially immortals."

Mary's voice trembled as she spoke. "It's true," she admitted. "That would work. But few mortals know about it. It is forbidden to speak of it in our world. We fear it."

"But you have a manuscript telling of its location?" Philip asked. "Then all we would need to do would be go there, come back, and find Magdalina."

"And destroy her." Rose stopped her pacing and looked around. "How far away is the Romani territory?"

"Let me see if I have a good map with me," Ethan said, reaching for his pack.

"I can see if Thad will give me some more information on how to get there," Theo offered.

"Are you seriously considering this?" Mary asked. "Dragons are dangerous."

"Sophia said it earlier: I can't be killed. Magdalina's curse has to be fulfilled," Rose told her. "I have nothing to lose, Mary."

"My magic won't work against dragons," she warned.

"I'd still like you along for company," Rose remarked softly.

Mary sighed. "You have it, Rose, and you know this. But I will be a burden to you without magic."

"We have much more than magic," Rose insisted. "Remember? We have faith, loyalty, and courage. You told me that before. You'll never convince me these things have done less for the world than magic."

Mary sank into a humble silence.

Rose sighed. "All right. We're going to do the impossible, possibly one last time. Who's in?"

"As always, my lady knight, you have in me a squire and blacksmith, at your service," Sophia saluted.

Ethan raised his hand. "You are my rescuer and leader. You have my tracking, hunting, and map-reading skills at your disposal."

Mary sighed. "For what it is worth, you have the magic of my friendship."

"It's worth a lot to me," Rose assured her. "What about you, Philip? Will you go to the Romani territory, slay a dragon, and face life-threatening danger with us, all to help break the curse placed on me?"

"Magdalina could very well come after my people next," he said. "I look to you, Lady Princess," he said, "to join our kingdoms together against evil." He smiled. "And I welcome the task to defend you from your curse as well."

"All right. I'll go and inform the King. You each need to go and prepare to depart in the morning. Sophia, gather extra supplies from the forage house. Mary, see if Fiona or Juana would like to come with us and gather your supplies. Ethan, get some grooms to ready my team of horses. Philip, go and collect your tournament winnings from the royal treasurer. My father will not be happy, but he is not known to cheat anyone. The money will help pay for our passage."

All of them agreed, and finishing their drinks, headed out of the tavern.

"What about me?" Theo called out from behind her.

"What about you?" Rose asked.

"Did you want me to come with you?" Theo asked. "You didn't ask me."

Rose stopped and placed her hand on his shoulder. "I'm sorry," she said, surprising him by her apology. "I didn't think I needed to. Throughout all the years we've been together, I have never needed to know if you would come with me. I just knew. But," she said as he tried to interrupt, "I know you have your own vengeance to pursue, and it is so close to where we are. If you want to stay behind, I understand."

He said nothing; he just looked at her, with that strange, enigmatic look of his.

He is going to make me ask, Rose thought, suddenly bitter. He is going to make me ask, just so he can say no and smooth it over with logic.

A thought popped into her mind. "Everon can be killed, too, with the dragon's blood."

He nodded. "I was thinking of that myself."

She sighed, impatient. There was nothing to be had, she decided. "So, will you come with me?"

He took her hand. "Where you go, I have always gone. Where you've stayed, I have stayed only a step behind. Your journey has always been my journey, and should you need me, I will be here for you."

Rose felt her heart nearly stop. "That was beautiful," she finally replied. "Thank you." I guess Philip's not the only one who is good at poetry, Rose admitted ruefully to herself.

"You're welcome."

Before she could say anything else, Philip came up beside her. "I've paid the bill, Rose," he told her. "Do you want us to meet you by the King's council room again?"

"What? Oh, uh, yes, that's a good idea," Rose said. She was still feeling the fervent beat of her heart as it clung to Theo's words.

She glanced around the room, as though seeing it for the first time. *How differently the world does look, when it is christened by hope.*

Looking from Theo to Philip, she grabbed them both by their arms. "Come on," she said. "We have work to do."

The music swelled around her and inside of her. A familiar tune caught her ears; it was the *Ballad of Queen Lucia,* an ode to her legend. And before Rose realized what she was doing, her voice broke free of its long imprisonment and soared along with the song.

> *Queen Lucia sought to love a special one*
> *Sir Benedict, his heart became the prize;*
> *He who was worthy of her love alone*
> *She saw as worthy in her own eyes.*

Rose, caught up in her own world, did not notice as Theo's fingers clenched around her arm even more tightly, nor did she notice how his breathing grew shallow as he lost the last of his carefully guarded heart was stolen.

Rose also did not notice on her other side as Philip, struck with shock at the pure clarity of her voice, nearly dropped her arm all together, as he stared at her in pure astonishment.

"What's wrong?" Rose asked, as she noticed both of Theo and Philip had stalled. "Did you lose something?"

"No," both of them said simultaneously.

As Rose turned back toward the door, returning to her plans as she pulled the two of them along, Theo glanced at over to see the unmoving wonder in Philip's gaze. One look at the prince, and Theo felt his initial wariness of the prince reignite.

Theo knew reality of allowing himself to dream of a life with the princess meant he had to acknowledge Philip for what he suddenly was: A rival.

18

,

"The King has taken ill, Your Highness."

Rose snorted at her father's valet. "I'm not surprised. Can you announce me anyway?"

"I am under direct orders not to allow anyone through without permission."

"I see how this is going to play out already," Rose muttered. It figures, she thought. Her father would find a way to circumvent any serious attempt of hers to lead the nation. "He's lucky all those in my council are away fulfilling their assignments. Announce me, please."

"I'll see if he can speak first, Your Highness."

The valet's dour look did nothing to deter her. Nor would she allow him to trample over her. She had a plan, and she was going to stick to it.

The valet returned shortly. "The King will see you now, Your Highness."

"Thank you." Rose walked past the man and into her father's chamber. She felt the rest of the world fold back under the pressure of her father's majestic surroundings.

The King was lying in his bed, his eyes closed as he pressed his palms into his temples.

"Your Majesty."

"Aurora."

Rose grimaced. "I prefer Rose, to be honest."

"Rose?" Stefanos looked confused. "Your middle name?"

"More or less. I began using it after I left home the first time," she explained. "Announcing you are a traveling foreign princess, or even a traveler who shares the name, just invites

147

trouble. But now I prefer Rose. I don't recognize the person Aurora would have grown up to be."

"That's a shame, for she loved her country more."

"Rose has learned there are other places in the world where love exists, and it exists there without the tinge of unhealthy pity," she mocked.

"You dare defy me? Openly?" Stefanos accused. "I could have you flogged for that."

"I'd take it as proper punishment, if the insult were indeed open," Rose countered. "We are in your private bedroom, and you are feigning ill to make sure no one else would bother you."

"I'm not playing make-believe, for goodness' sake."

Rose smirked. "Shall I send for Reverend Thorne?"

"I'll not let Rhone live without a rightful ruler."

"I am the rightful ruler," Rose insisted. "You said it yourself. I was destined to save the kingdom, and I mean to save it from evil as much as from you."

"Ungrateful girl," Stefanos grumbled into his pillow. "You wound me with your words."

"Well, you've assured me of your purpose enough to know my words will not be fatal." Rose took a step closer. "I have an answer to your ultimatum. I am going to kill Magdalina."

"What?" Stefanos shot up straight in his bed, looking much more like a lonely, little boy than a king of a grand kingdom.

"My friends and I depart at dawn," she said. "We are going to go and find a way to destroy her. If we can kill her, we might be able to break the curse."

"I've tried for years to do just that. No one comes back alive. It's a fool's errand, Aurora."

"Rose," she corrected. "Magdalina told me I have made my curse a blessing in my own right. I have decided she is right, and I will test her on her claim. If her curse is to be fulfilled, she will be unable to kill me."

"You're mad."

"Determined." Rose smirked. "That is my decision."

"What if you should fail?"

"I needn't worry about the throne. Isra or Ronan can rule in my place. Both of your other children have been taught to fight and survive, and, while they are not supposed to inherit the throne over me, both can lead."

The King paused. "Do you like your siblings, Aurora?" Stefanos asked.

"Yes. Of course," Rose replied. "Why?"

"You would leave them to clean up the evil you leave behind?"

"No one is guaranteed a life without opposition or evil," Rose shot back. "The important thing is you teach them to watch for it, to recognize it, and to have the courage to stand up against it." She took a step closer. "One would think you would agree with me, considering my life has been all about answering for your own mistakes. This way, should I kill her, even if the curse is not broken, she will be unable to harm anyone else."

Stefanos frowned, anger crossing his features. He sat up and grabbed a quill and a sheet of parchment from his nearby desk. "I will let you go," he said, surprising her, as he scribbled furiously on the paper. "But only on one condition. You will sign a letter saying that, on the day after your eighteenth birthday, you will abdicate the throne."

"But if I break the curse—"

"Then you will be awake to tear up the contract," the King interrupted. He handed her the piece of paper. "There. Read through and sign it, and I will send you off with money, supplies, whatever you need, and a guard to go behind you. Captain Locke will no doubt be eager to follow you once more. He hates town life."

"But–"

"Sign it. Sign it with the pen, and then seal it with your blood, Aurora. What can it hurt you? What can you lose?"

She looked at the paper and read the words; she blinked, as though they had been written in a different language.

I, Aurora, Princess of Rhone, give up the throne to the kingdom on this day, the day after my eighteenth birthday, and resign my say in all kingdom matters and the subsequent consequences.

Rose sighed. "Fine." With her scrawl of a signature and a drop of her blood later, she turned toward the door while Stefanos returned to his bed. She watched as he rolled up the scroll and tucked it into his sleeve. Suddenly, she frowned. "What do you mean by 'subsequent consequences?'"

"We'll know more clearly when it happens," Stefanos muttered. "I can't say for certain at the present."

"But you do mean that Isra will take the throne, right?" Rose asked. "She's the older twin."

"We'll have to see," the King repeated.

Rose faltered as she headed toward the door. "Just what did you do to Magdalina," she asked, "that made her hate you so?"

He was quiet for a long moment; Rose almost thought he wouldn't answer the question. "She blames me for the Magdust trade," Stefanos said with a sigh.

"Why would she blame you?" Rose frowned. "It's not like it is legal in the kingdom."

150

"Who is to say why she blames me? A king must take responsibility for his kingdom; that's all I can say to that."

"But you didn't take responsibility for any of this," Rose corrected. "I did. I wonder why."

"There's nothing more important to me than the crown and our family. She took you away and left the shell of the promise of my most dearly held wish. Who is to say Magdalina won't send her armies to kill Isra, too, taking all the royal children away from me and Rhone?"

He turned his face into his pillow and began to weep, something Rose never would have thought he would do.

19

⁺⸴⁺

Thad was lighting the candles along the church pews when Theo walked in.

"When are you leaving?" Thad called out, his voice seeming louder than normal as it echoed through the empty sanctuary.

"I don't know how you know me so well," Theo said with a sad half-smile.

"I would have thought it was obvious, given our last conversation." Thad put down the flame he carried and headed over to his brother. "So tell me the plan."

Theo quickly told his brother of their plans. "Rose is determined to kill Magdalina," Theo explained. "She thinks the dragon blood will break the blood seal on the curse."

"As much as he would say in public he is against it, I think the Grand Father would secretly approve," Thad said. "So I will make arrangements for a special blessing for your travels in the morning."

"Rose won't come." Theo said it with a hidden bitterness. "She thinks God has abandoned her, left her to a cursed fate."

"So do all who see such times."

Theo sighed. "We'll probably leave out early, anyway. But thanks for the offer."

"The offer is not for you, brother," Thad replied. "Prayer is not for the people who would only pray for themselves." He smiled. "I will do what I can for you, and that includes, I will shamelessly admit, the comfort of praying for you here."

"I'm really happy to hear you say that, brother," Theo said with a sly grin on his face. "Because I have a couple of books and scrolls I need to borrow from you."

Thad's face fell.

20

∴

The sharp, cold morning air was in direct contrast to the warm pub and the soft bed she would leave behind, but Rose knew it was for the best. She was seventeen years old now, at last, on the brink of adulthood.

Her hair was freshly trimmed, her armor was polished, and her bags were packed. After finishing her preparation for her departure, she had spent the night looking out of her tower window, wondering if all the world was so peaceful at night.

She'd watched the sunrise peer out over the high, green mountains of Rhone, their color growing from the darkest of forest greens to shining emeralds, rivaling even the hue of Theo's eyes.

She turned to him now, as he mounted on his horse. "Do you remember the first day we set out last time?" she asked.

Theo fixed the straps of the pack he wore on his back, which held the precious manuscripts Thad had been reluctant, but resigned, to hand over. Rose was glad to hear Theo had managed to get Queen Lucia's story, as well as Magdalina's, in addition to as much information about the Romani language and history as possible. "Of course. You asked me if I was ready to begin training to be a knight."

"You replied by saying, 'I already am one, just an untrained one.'" Rose smiled. "I always liked that."

"I never told you, but that was the answer I gave to my grandfather, Reverend Thorne, when he inducted Thad and me into the church. Contrary to what most people think, there are a lot of similarities between priesthood and knighthood."

"Really?"

"Yes. Both seek to fulfill a higher calling on their lives, both do what they can, when they can, and both require ongoing training, patience, and growth." He grinned at her. "Especially where you're concerned, Rosary."

She laughed, glad to feel her heart lighten.

"Are you ready to leave?"

Rose turned at the sound of Isra's voice. "Isra. I didn't think you would–"

"What? Notice you were gone?" Isra rolled her eyes. "I've lived too long in your shadow, Rose. If you are gone, I run from daylight." She shook back her long, dark hair. "I also came to remind you to write to me this time."

"I will try," Rose muttered, already making up the necessary excuses in her mind.

"I know Theo will still write to me," she warned. "And I'm hoping Philip will, too."

"Philip?"

"Of course," Isra said with a teasing sigh and a small blush. "He's such a good poet, you know. I'm hoping to read some of it."

"I'll see that he writes to you then, if nothing else. I'm sure Virtue won't mind the extra letters." Rose glanced behind her to see her faithful falcon sitting peacefully on the back of her saddle pack.

"See that you do. You owe me, you know."

"For what?" Rose asked.

"For keeping an eye out for the King and Queen, of course," Isra told her. She lowered her voice. "The King told you, did he not, that there are secrets every ruler has kept, right? Well, I mean to discover them."

ONCE UPON A PRINCESS

Rose bit back a smile, realizing Isra had been diligent to keep her watch on their father throughout the night, even to the point of spying. "You always were a better scholar than I was," Rose said, giving her younger sister an approving smile. "You'd probably make a much better queen, too."

"Of course I would. But that's only because I don't actually have to be the queen. People are always better at things they don't do than the people who do them."

Rose laughed and reached down and gripped her sister's hand in her own. "I promise, I'll take you with me on my next journey," she said.

"I'm counting on it, considering I will be likely committing treason for you in the coming weeks," Isra said. "You know how secretive the King is, and how blatant his apathy is for Ronan and myself. If he catches me in his study, he'll probably have no qualms about throwing me in the dungeon."

Rose was surprised. "I don't think he'd do that. He is very concerned with keeping the people happy."

"Mama says it is because he wasn't born into the throne. He wants to keep it very badly."

"Well, he will. He has me, and you and Ronan. One would think he would be content with three heirs."

"He doesn't like any of us, Rose."

"He doesn't know any of us."

"He doesn't want to."

Rose bit her lip. "I don't know what to say to that," she said, admitting defeat. "But if what you say is true, then you must promise me you will be extra careful."

"Only if you promise me the same," Isra demanded.

"I will. You have my word."

"Fine. I accept. And I will accept with the same enthusiasm and undercurrent of deliberate deceit." Isra smirked. "I can already tell you will find some kind of way to justify getting nearly killed."

"Don't worry for her, Isra," Philip spoke up, as his horse came up next to Rose. "I will be watching out for your sister."

Isra snickered. "Then I can rest much better," she assured him, "with the bare assurance your poetry will be the one to eulogize her."

"Absolutely," Philip promised, making Isra laugh once more. "If you feel I must, I shall write it ahead of time."

"So long as you write to me consistently," Isra said, batting her eyes in a flirtatious manner. "Goodness knows Rose is terrible about correspondence."

"I will," Philip promised. "I will write so much Virtue will need a whole day off to recover from his deliveries."

"Don't even think about making Virtue suffer any," Rose objected, reaching behind her to stroke her falcon's feathers while Philip and Isra laughed.

Sophia and Ethan came to meet them, mounted and ready. Mary, still sleepy, was curled up on Ethan's shoulder, under the protection of his dark hood. A small band of guards, including Captain Locke and Roderick, had gathered in the distance, waiting for her signal, no doubt once more sent out by the Queen.

"We're ready with the armor and weapons, Rose," Sophia called.

"Excellent. Ethan?"

"Food and supplies are accounted for."

"Good. I guess Mary's still tired."

"She was up most of the night talking with Fiona and Juana," Isra spoke up. "You can't blame her for wanting to spend time with her cousins."

"No, I can't," Rose agreed. "Hopefully her healing herbs and potions are all packed."

"They should be," Ethan told her. "I saw her put them in when I was getting the food stored."

"All right. We'll risk it, if nothing else. We should be safe till we leave Rhonian land." Rose turned her attention to Philip. "How's the money?"

"Plenty to go around," he told her.

"And Theo, I know you have the scrolls from Thad. Anything else you are in charge of?"

"All the prayers have been said," Theo said, nodding his head down toward her wrist, where the rosary beads he had given her remained carefully wrapped.

"Wonderful. All right then." Rose looked tenderly at each of the ones who had willingly trusted themselves into her care–plucky Sophia, with her iron will; gentle Ethan, young and precocious; Mary, faithful and also faithfully innovative; Philip, the newcomer, with a penchant for adventure, and apparently poetry; and Theo, her best friend and proven providence, his soul only marred by the desire for revenge, yet somehow brightened because of it.

These were her friends, her followers, her family. "Ready to go slay a dragon?"

C. S. Johnson is the author of several young adult sci-fi and fantasy novels, including *The Starlight Chronicles* series, the *Once Upon a Princess* saga, and the *Divine Space Pirates* trilogy. She currently lives in Atlanta with her family.

AUTHOR'S NOTE AND ACKNOWLEDGEMENTS

Dear Reader,

Welcome to the new world of my new series. I've many more I wish to explore yet, but this is one of the easier ones to slip into. If you have enjoyed my *Starlight Chronicles* series, you might be surprised by the departure in my style; it's still there, of course, but the voice has changed.

But then, Rose is very different from my other protagonist. Hamilton lives in a world where he thinks he is able to hold off on growing up, even as he does, while Rose has learned to grow up very quickly, even as she can't.

Still, I am hoping you like her as much you've enjoyed Hamilton (or will enjoy, because obviously you're going to buy my other books now that you've read this). God works his magic in our lives in mysterious, ironic, silly, and seemingly frivolous ways as much through pain, and usually through people. And it's my blessing in getting to bring some of those people to life, even while reaffirming or challenging elements of yours.

I thank you so much for your support in recent months. Life has calmed down a bit; my goals are more focused, and my time is more flexible. There is nothing more I desire than getting to write more and to interact with you more.

Finally, I'm going to ask nicely if you would leave a review for my book. I'm not asking for you to blast it out over social media, or tattoo it on your chest, or write it on your car. Every review helps, and I do tend to read them, especially at my worst moments.

Please check back in with Rose in the next book in the saga, *Beauty's Quest (Once Upon a Princess,* Part II).

Until We Meet Again,

C. S. Johnson

OTHER WORKS BY OTHER DIRE WOLF AUTHORS

 *Wolf Code: A Sheltering Wilderness*

Chandler Brett

A college student, Don, finds his dream career is at odds with the ideals his newfound love interest holds, even as his choices affect the survival chances for a pack of wolves. Check for more information at www.direwolfbooks.com.

 *The Adventures of Shamis and Larry*

Jeff Sartini

An off-beat fairy tale adventure ensues as Shamis and Larry head off with a magical mule and a one-headed monkey. Check for more information at www.direwolfbooks.com.

SAMPLE READING

Chapter 1 *from*

BEAUTY'S QUEST

PART II OF THE *ONCE UPON A PRINCESS* SAGA

❉ ❉ ❉ ❉

C. S. Johnson

Courtesy of

www.direwolfbooks.com

DIREWOLF
— BOOKS —

ONCE UPON A PRINCESS

ONCE UPON A PRINCESS

1

If there was one thing Princess Aurora Rosemarie Mohanagan knew, it was that she had no reason to fear death. But as she glanced down at the half-sunk ship, wrecked on the rocky coast below her, Rose admitted to herself—more than a little reluctantly—she was lucky she'd survived.

"It's a miracle we're alive, Rose." The small fairy perched on her shoulder echoed Rose's thoughts as they both looked toward the harbor.

Rose tried not to smile as she watched Mary, her small fairy friend, wring the excess water out from the folds of her dress. "You're right about that, Mary. But I don't know if *they* think so," Rose muttered, nodding down to the gruff sea captain and his crew. She watched them as they waded into the cove, pulling the storm-weathered bow of the vessel closer to shore. "Philip gave them quite a lecture."

"One they won't likely be forgetting anytime soon, either," Philip agreed.

Rose looked over to see Prince Philip of Einish, her newest friend and traveling companion, making his way up the rocky beach. His copper-brown hair glistened with seawater, the droplets sliding down his sunburned face and into his beard. "Oh really?" she teased. "What did you tell him?"

"I told him the truth," Philip assured her with a grim smile. "I told him he'd almost killed two royals, and neither country would be happy to accept his calls to port anymore should anything adverse happen." He stepped up next to her. "I'm sure neither your father nor my brother would object to keeping them from our countries' docks after their incompetence during that storm."

"Einish and Rhone do make quite a large profit from the sea-faring trade," Ethan, the youngest of the group, spoke up. He sighed as he looked at the soaking wet packs in his hand, the remnants of his precious manuscripts and scrolls. "Even

164

when Sophia and I were living with our family"—his lips tightened at the memory—"I'd never known my father to complain of an investment failing when it came to trading with either."

Rose agreed. The kingdom of Rhone, her home, was mostly landlocked, but the few harbors it had on the northern side of the kingdom were bustling with activity throughout the year. She remembered seeing several when she had been younger, on one of her grand tours of the nation, the feeling of awe as she surveyed Elis, Rhone's largest port, and she watched the people there, busy about the docks. She knew Philip's warning was no light threat.

Looking at the sullen expression on Ethan's face, Rose turned her attention back to the situation at hand. "Where is Sophia?" she asked. She lifted her hand up to shield herself from the streaming sunlight as she looked around for her squire. "I thought I saw her make her way to the shore a few moments ago."

"She is a good swimmer," Ethan reminded Rose. "She might just be lingering to see if she can help. Theo was doing that, too."

"Well, I know he was going to help with the burials for the two crew members who died." Rose's fists clenched again. The reality of coming so close to a watery grave made her shiver. "I hope they're not making him help dig graves."

"I doubt it," Philip said with a sad sigh. "I know the men are going to be given a burial at sea. Many feel it is more appropriate, considering they drowned."

"I suppose so," Rose grimly agreed. "If that's what they're doing, then Theo should be here soon."

"All in a day's work for a priest, right?" Philip asked, shaking the water out of his gloves.

Rose snorted disdainfully. "Just because he was raised in the church and knows how to perform rites and catechisms and the like doesn't mean he's a priest." She glanced over Philip's shoulder to see if she could spot her long-time friend coming up from the beach.

"He acts like it enough," Philip reminded her.

"But he's still not, so get it right." Rose stuck her tongue out at him before turning her attention elsewhere. "If he was a full priest, maybe he could have stopped the rain sooner."

"It wasn't that long of a storm."

"*To you*, maybe it wasn't that long of a storm," Rose muttered. "When that storm grew severe, it had to have been already raining for at least two weeks."

Mary chuckled, her small wings fanning Rose's face. "It just seemed like two weeks," she said. "It was really only about four days, Rose."

"I lost track of time as soon as the crew stopped listening to reason," Rose said. "Especially after those goons in charge of the ship were trying to puff the sails to catch *more* of the wind, rather than pulling it up." She gave Mary a tiny pat on her head, flicking Mary's dark ginger locks affectionately. "If you hadn't used your magic to find this island, I don't know what we would have done."

"We'd probably be swimming back to Rhone. Or maybe we could've tried to get closer to the mainland, where the Romani territory is. We've got to be at least halfway there."

"Don't think I wouldn't completely object to it, either. I suppose now we will have to find a way to get more supplies." Rose turned to Philip. "How much money do we have left?"

"A good bit. But Rhonian money is different from the money used in the Peloponnesian countries," Philip warned her.

"Too bad we don't deal in Magdust," Ethan said as he began to move higher on the rocks, looking for a place to air out the parchment he'd rescued from his drenched pack. "I'll bet *that* would get us some money pretty quick."

"Don't say such things." Rose's admonishment came swiftly but softly. "Especially when you're working with Thad's manuscripts." Theo and Thad's parents had been killed by Everon, Magdalina's son, in connection with the illegal Magdust trade in Rhone. Theo wouldn't have appreciated that comment, Rose thought.

"I was just trying to liven things up some," Ethan grumbled, rubbing his hand through his shaggy brown hair. "I didn't mean any harm."

"I should hope so," Mary scoffed. "I've had friends who have been killed and smashed into Magdust."

"What?" Rose was shocked. "You've never mentioned that to me." Mary was loyal to Rose and her party, and one of the only fairies, in all of Rhone who still supported the ruling family. Rose could not remember a time her life had not been touched with Mary's devotion.

Mary shrugged. "You know I have never held the Magdust trade against you, Rose. I wouldn't want you to think that, especially with Magdalina placing that curse on you."

"I would never think of you the way I think of Magdalina. Being a fairy has nothing to do with being evil," Rose assured her. She turned back to look over the edge of the rocky cliffs. "Mary, can you help Ethan with the maps and scrolls? They need to be dried."

"No problem," Mary murmured dutifully.

Philip came up next to her. "Can I help you with anything?"

"Yes," Rose replied. "Please take an inventory of our remaining supplies, and count how much money we do have so we can see about moving on toward the Romani territory."

"Sure thing."

Rose sighed softly as Philip headed back down to the shore. She was alone for the moment.

Rose inhaled deeply, feeling the salty sweetness of the air. The beach was beautiful, with its white sand kissing the sea with such tenderness. There was a calmness in the air she would have given anything to have had during the nighttime storms. Rose knew full well she should have been grateful, even relaxed, to be on such lovely, solid dry land after several weeks of traveling by sea.

But she wasn't.

ONCE UPON A PRINCESS

Another victory for Magdalina, she thought, feeling the full weight of the curse placed on her at infancy. Like all the previous royal heirs of Rhone, Rose had been blessed by the gifts of the fairies, Fiona and Juana, Mary's older cousins, at the celebration of her birth. But before Mary could give her a touch of magic as well, Magdalina showed up, angry at not being invited and bitter against the kingdom. It was then she had cursed Rose to prick her finger on the spindle of a spinning wheel and die on her eighteenth birthday, now less than a year away. Magdalina had then laughed and took her leave.

Mary had been able to alter the curse—death-like sleep would replace death—but that was little comfort to Rose. It was still the end of her life.

Rose looked down at her palms, her gaze tracing up and down the length of her fingers, as she wondered which one would betray her.

After seeing Magdalina at her royal birthday party just over three months before, and feeling every second as it counted down to her eighteenth birthday, Rose knew more than ever she had to find a way to break the curse. That had been the plan when they'd set off from Rhone.

Now, if she was going to get the dragon's blood she needed to take care of Magdalina, she had to find a way off this prison of an island—and fast.

She pressed her fingers into her temples, steeling herself against the fear that clutched at her heart; the terror squeezed the beauty of her surroundings out of sight, until only the ugliness of despair and the unknown remained.

"It'll be all right, Rosary."

Rose jumped at the sudden presence by her side. She looked over to see Theo had climbed up next to her. "I know," she said, aware she was half-lying. "But we are only about halfway to Romani territory, and we can't afford to be delayed long."

"We've made good time," Theo told her. "We are on the island of Maltia, according to the men from the ship. There's

a city on the other side of that peak over there." He pointed
to a mountaintop in the distance. "We should be able to find
a church there, according to some of the crew. I'll be able to
see about securing us quarters. And hopefully, passage on
another ship as well."

"Are you sure you can trust their information?" Rose asked,
nodding back to the sailors. "After the confusion on the ship,
I'd rather not."

"A lot of them are superstitious men." Theo shrugged.
"But they are not as given to fancy when it comes to knowing
their trade and its routes."

"We're not going to have to wait for them, are we?" Rose
asked.

Theo gazed at her, his emerald-colored eyes
complementing the comfort of the sea. "We don't have to
wait for repairs, if repairs are even possible. According to a
man who'd talked to Captain Locke, the Maltians have a
special trade route for the Romani territory."

"Good." Rose sighed. "Now we just have to get the money
for supplies and passage."

"We'll find a way to get it," Theo assured her. "Don't lose
hope, Rose. This could be a good thing. Maybe we'll be able
to find out more about the dragons."

"I'll try. No promises."

Theo smiled. "That's the Rose I know."

"Right now, Philip's checking supplies while Ethan and
Mary are working on drying out the scrolls Thad gave us."

"They're not damaged, are they?" Theo's eyes were wide
with sudden concern.

Rose knew Theo's older brother, who resided in the chapel
in Rhone's capital city of Havilah, probably prayed just as
much for the safe return of his manuscripts and scrolls as he
did for the safe return of Theo and his friends. "I think Mary
will be able to take care of it," she told him.

"That's good." Theo breathed a sigh of relief. "My brother
is a forgiving sort, but I'd hate to be the one who tests his
limits."

As Rose laughed, a wink of light flickered in the corner of her eye. She turned to see Sophia, her thirteen-year-old squire, as she sloshed onto the beach below.

"Did you finish taking care of those who died?" Rose asked.

"Yes, both of them. The older was a man who had been seafaring since he was eight, and the younger not even a year behind Ethan."

Rose reached out and placed her hand on his arm. She started to say something, but she found she had no words to say. It took a moment before she felt him relax as he let himself be comforted. She knew his heart was shaken, and his body had yet to catch up to the shock of seeing the dead. Rose had a feeling he would never be completely familiar with it, no matter his education as a priest or his training as a knight.

He drew up his arm, allowing Rose's hand to fall into his. His fingers tightened around hers. "Thanks, Rosary."

Theo smiled a bit as he momentarily fiddled with the chain of rosary beads at her wrist; he'd given them to her shortly before they had departed from Rhone.

"We should start heading to the city. The rain's let up, but nightfall will be here before we know it."

"Yes," she agreed. "Let's get the others."

Thank you for reading! Please leave a review for this book and check for other books and updates!